A Candlelight Ecstasy Romance

"QUITE A LITTLE DANCE YOU PUT ON FOR MY FRIENDS TONIGHT," CHUCK SAID COLDLY.

Faye's eyes narrowed. "Yes, it was, and it was a beautiful and sensual dance. And I'm tired of defending myself. Look, Chuck, we're not arguing about my belly dancing, and we both know it."

"Yes, we are," he protested. "We're arguing about the way you flaunt yourself in front of other men when you belly dance."

"No, we're not. It's the way you feel when I get up there and show that I'm a very sensual woman—that's the problem. You don't like it one bit. I threaten you." Faye knew she had struck a nerve.

"So you think you threaten me, do you? Well, why don't I make love to you and see just how threatening I find you?" Chuck demanded, reaching out to pull her to him, claiming her lips with a kiss.

CANDLELIGHT ECSTASY ROMANCES®

SURPRISE PACKAGE

Emily Elliott

A CANDLELIGHT ECSTASY ROMANCE™

Published by
Dell Publishing Co., Inc.
1 Dag Hammarskjold Plaza
New York, New York 10017

Dell ® TM 681510, Dell Publishing Co., Inc.
Candlelight Ecstasy Romance®, 1,203,540, is a registered
trademark of Dell Publishing Co., Inc., New York, New York.

ISBN: 0-440-18374-X

Printed in the United States of America
First printing—June 1985

To Our Readers:

We have been delighted with your enthusiastic response to Candlelight Ecstasy Romances®, and we thank you for the interest you have shown in this exciting series.

In the upcoming months we will continue to present the distinctive sensuous love stories you have come to expect only from Ecstasy. We look forward to bringing you many more books from your favorite authors and also the very finest work from new authors of contemporary romantic fiction.

As always, we are striving to present the unique, absorbing love stories that you enjoy most—books that are more than ordinary romance. Your suggestions and comments are always welcome. Please write to us at the address below.

Sincerely,

The Editors
Candlelight Romances
1 Dag Hammarskjold Plaza
New York, New York 10017

CHAPTER ONE

Chuck Goodall pushed his horn-rimmed glasses back up on his nose and sipped his drink quietly, letting the sounds of stereo music and masculine laughter wash over him in waves. He gazed around the room at his college fraternity brothers and wondered how on earth Ray Donovan had gotten so many of them together, so many years and so many miles from the frat house they had shared at the University of Texas.

He noted that Harry was sporting quite a paunch, and that Roger had a bald spot on the back of his head. I guess I haven't done so badly after all, he thought as he ran his fingers through his thick brown hair, only faintly touched with gray, then glanced at his relatively flat waistline and over at the big birthday cake that graced Ray's dining room table. The cake was for Chuck. In fact, the whole party was for him, but Chuck would have been just as happy if Ray had skipped the whole thing.

"Hey, Chuck, let me fix you another drink!" Ray said as he upended the last of his Tequila Sunrise and motioned for Chuck to do the same to his Scotch and soda. "Come on, drink up! It's your birthday and you're letting the rest of us drink you under the table."

"Sorry, I'll try to catch up," Chuck said, and took a huge swallow of the smooth Scotch, letting the drink trickle slowly down the back of his throat. It stung a little, but it felt good as it hit his stomach. Maybe Ray was right, he thought. He needed to celebrate. After all, tax season was over and he would be working much shorter hours for the next few months. He finished his drink and handed his glass to Ray. "Okay, old buddy. You have me convinced. Get me another drink."

Ray nodded and got up, his gait still steady after a number of the potent Tequila Sunrises that he was so fond of, but Chuck wondered how long it would be before Ray was visibly drunk. At least Ray wouldn't have to drive home, he thought, since this was his house. Ray didn't get to party that much these days, he mused, not between his long hours as a partner in the accounting firm where they both worked and a beautiful wife and three kids at home. So when Ray did have a chance to kick up his heels, he tended to do it with a vengeance.

But a birthday party with all his old fraternity buddies? Chuck wondered. Wasn't that going a little out of the way? If Ray had wanted to give him a stag party, he could have invited the other members of their accounting firm. He didn't have to call all over the country and drag their old frat brothers to Houston, although most of them didn't look as though attending the party had been much of a sacrifice.

Chuck looked down at his left hand, bare after so many years of wearing the band Julie had put on his finger, and smiled grimly. More than one of his old frat brothers had congratulated him on his newfound freedom, joking that in divorcing his wife of ten years he'd rejoined the world of the living. What would this bunch think if they knew the truth about why he was single again? he wondered.

Ray returned with a drink in each hand and handed one

to Chuck. He plopped down on one side of Chuck. Danny Miller sat on the other side.

"So how's the swinging life?" Danny asked as Chuck sipped his drink. "Are you enjoying all those hot-blooded young things out there?" Danny had divorced a couple of years ago and had thoroughly enjoyed the single life before he remarried.

Chuck shrugged. "I haven't really had time to find out," he admitted. "The divorce wasn't final until I was into tax season."

Danny lit a cigarette and shook his head. "Don't tell me you waited for the divorce to go through before you started going out." He took a deep drag on his cigarette and smiled as he exhaled. "You haven't changed a bit, have you?" he asked. "Same old Chuck. Straight-arrow if there ever was one."

Chuck hid a flash of annoyance and nodded. "I'm afraid so," he said. "There have to be a few of us in the world so the rest of you can enjoy feeling wild."

Ray laughed out loud. "Well, now that your divorce is final, I hope you'll take advantage of it," he said, and sipped his drink. "Now that Jerry Tanner's gone and got married, there's nobody at work to razz about their love life, you know? Everybody's married."

"What about the new accountant you said you were getting?" Danny asked as he crushed his cigarette in the ashtray. "Is he single?"

Ray grinned wickedly and slapped Chuck's knee with his palm. "He's nothing. He's a she, and she is most definitely single. And Chuckie-boy here is the lucky devil who gets to work with her."

"Hey, did I hear you say you're getting a new lady accountant?" Jim Meredith asked as he perched on the edge

9

of the couch. Jim was an accountant in a prestigious firm in Dallas. "Who are you getting?"

Chuck sipped his drink before answering. "I've never met the lady, but her name's Faye Catalini and she comes to us highly recommended," he said.

"What's she going to be doing?" Jim asked.

"Tax manager," Chuck replied.

"What does she look like?" Danny demanded. "Tall? Skinny? Buckteeth? Orthopedic shoes? Does she have a face like a horse?"

Ray, Jim, and Chuck roared with laughter. "You can tell he's not out in the business world these days!" Ray snickered. Danny was a construction engineer and seldom saw the inside of an office.

"Yeah, you ought to see some of the knockouts that inhabit those little dress-for-success suits," Chuck added.

"And let me tell you, Faye Catalini is one of them," Robert Jonas chimed in as he sat down on the edge of the coffee table, just as he used to do in the frat house. "She's one hell of a looker."

"How would you know?" Ray demanded. "You're not an accountant."

"No, but she did my business returns a couple of years ago at the office," Robert said. "I thought a couple of my cardiac patients were going to have coronaries right there in the waiting room when she would walk through."

"Real little hot piece, huh?" Danny asked eagerly. Chuck sipped his drink and tried not to appear as interested as he was.

Robert snorted. "I wish! The lady was beautiful all right, but as cold and businesslike as the calculator in her briefcase. She was there for one purpose, and that was to do my taxes. That was all."

"Aww, what a shame," Ray teased. "You're so deprived. You're only making it with your wife and your reception-ist." It was a well-known fact that Robert's receptionist had also been his mistress for several years.

The men all laughed and Robert launched into the tale of one of his weekends out of town with his mistress. Chuck sat quietly, laughing at the right spots as he half listened to Robert's sexploits. So the new accountant was a no-nonsense knockout, he thought as he sipped his drink.

In the last few years, since the world of accounting had opened up to women, there were more and more women entering the field, and many of them were doing quite well. But it was unusual for a woman to reach managerial level by the age of thirty, which was the age Faye's résumé had said she was. It seemed to Chuck that many of the prettier women on the way up in business got sidetracked by dat-ing and marriage.

Chuck finished his drink and glanced at the big birthday cake that Ray had said they would cut at eleven. It was ten thirty. *Why is it so important to cut the cake exactly at eleven?* Chuck wondered as he mixed himself another drink in the kitchen. It wasn't like Ray to plan a party so carefully.

Hesitant to rejoin the noisy party, Chuck leaned against the kitchen counter and sipped his drink. So Faye Catalini was all business on the job, he thought, even though she was a knockout. Well, that suited him just fine. The last thing he needed was to have a sexy siren in the office! That kind just did not mix with the conservative world of ac-counting, he mused, snapping out of it when he heard a car pull up in front of the house. Better go see who else came to wish me well, he thought as he headed back to the living room, carrying his drink with him.

Chuck looked around for a new face. He spotted no one new, but found most of the party engaged in a dirty-joke-telling contest. Honestly, this bunch never changes, he thought as he wondered again why Ray hadn't invited any of their fellow accountants to the get-together. Even though Ray frequently voiced the opinion that most of their colleagues were dreary bores, he usually included them when he had a party.

Chuck listened to one ribald joke after another. The jokes broke off when Ray brought out three huge candles, five small ones and one medium-size candle for good luck, placing them around the birthday cake and lighting them. He motioned to Chuck, but just as Chuck approached the dining room table the lights in the living room dimmed suddenly and the stereo became silent, throwing the room into a darkened hush. The dim table lamps and the flickering candles provided the only illumination, and the quiet murmur of men's voices the only sound in the room. Chuck could feel the hair rise on the back of his neck. What on earth was going on?

The woman who stood in the small foyer listened for the music that would signal her entrance into the crowded living room. She shook out her hair and tucked one of her flowing scarves a little more securely into her low-cut costume top. She raised her arms slowly, finger cymbals in her hands, her heart pumping as she waited for the haunting, throbbing music. She didn't move her hips, since the tinkling of brass coins suspended from her skirt would alert the man at the end of the room. One of the men who had greeted her had pointed out the guest of honor, but all she could see in the dimly lit room was a tall man with horn-rimmed glasses. Well, she would see him a little closer when she danced for him, she thought. Rubbing one slippered foot against the other, she took a deep breath, waiting for her cue.

Chuck jumped a little when the first chord of the strange-sounding music leapt from the stereo, but at that moment the door to the living room opened and the music was forgotten. Chuck drew in his breath when he caught sight of the exotic woman who was whirling, no, *dancing*, into the room, her skirt and scarves billowing around her, finger cymbals clicking to the provocative rhythm of the strange music on the stereo. She had a mass of wildly curling black hair that fell in a cascade nearly to her waist, and her almond-shaped eyes were dark and mysterious, hinting at provocative secrets. Chuck was drawn to the perfect symmetry of the body that was undulating into the room. The woman's full breasts and wide hips suggested a sensuality that took his breath away.

Swinging, bouncing, she quickly danced to the middle of the room. Her arms, legs, and shoulders all moved as she kept pace with the pounding rhythm, her hips grinding to the beat of the music, the coins on her skirt and bodice bouncing as her hands swayed around her head. Chuck's throat went dry as her hips bounced in one direction and her breasts in the other, and his eyes were glued to the fluid motions of her graceful body.

Standing mesmerized by the dining room table, a slow, embarrassed blush crept up his neck and his face. She was a belly dancer! They had hired a belly dancer to dance for him tonight. No wonder Ray hadn't invited any of their fellow accountants! Chuck stared at the woman, embarrassment and astonishment in his expression. She was putting on this dance just for him!

Ah, this is bliss, the woman thought as she moved in tandem with the music, following the steps she had always

13

known and making up more as she went along. She let herself get caught up in the sensual sway of the old Arabian melody that wrapped itself around her and led her where it would. She tossed her wildly curled hair around and drew out one of her scarves, winding it around her body and then letting it drift around her arms and legs before tossing it over to one of the men on the couch. Throwing her head back, she moved in time with the music, her face and her arms and the feminine parts of her body a graceful tribute to her womanliness.

How does she do it? Chuck asked himself as she executed one particularly fascinating contortion. How can she get her body to do those things? He stared, mesmerized, stunned by the mystery and the sensual appeal of her body and her bearing. She moved with the music, her face exotic and inviting, but the sensuality seemed to be strictly private, even when she was dancing close to one man or another. But intense enchantment was there, emanating from every pore of the woman.

Slowly, as the music slowed and her movements became less frenzied, Chuck felt himself less embarrassed that she was dancing for him and more and more aware of the deep sensuality that her movements revealed. Yet her movements were not suggestive, he thought, or lewd, or in any way risqué. They were beautiful. Truly beautiful. And suddenly Chuck felt himself in the grip of desire so strong he could taste it. He wanted this woman, whoever she was. Oh, how he wanted her!

Chuck jumped when Ray tapped him on the shoulder. "Fantastic, huh?"

"Who is she?" Chuck whispered, his eyes not leaving the woman.

Ray shrugged. "She goes by the name Fatima." Ray

turned back to the dancer, and together they watched Fatima as the music slowed and she slowed with it. She began to dance her way across the room, and suddenly her dark eyes looked up and caught Chuck's. He stared into their depths, his heart pounding as she held his gaze boldly.

Fatima stared into the big hazel eyes that looked at her from behind thick horn-rimmed glasses. He stared back at her steadily, showing none of the astonishment or embarrassment he had exhibited earlier, when she had begun her dance. Now, she read desire there, desire and need and a kind of wistfulness, making his big hazel eyes touchingly vulnerable. Without breaking eye contact, she danced over to him and moved around him in a semicircle, her shoulders and arms swaying with the graceful sensuality of a snake. This close, she could smell his after-shave and feel the heat of his body, and she had an inexplicable urge to toss her scarf around his neck and draw his head close to hers.

As Fatima danced away from him, her musky perfume tantalized his nostrils and the swinging of her dangling earrings hypnotized him. Her facial features were not too distinct in the dim candlelight, but he thought he saw firm wide lips, and a beauty mark on her temple. I would kill at this moment to have her, he thought as her hips swayed provocatively to the haunting pulse of the music.

Fatima changed her movements as the slow, haunting music seemed to reach out and seduce her soul. She swayed and rocked to the sad strains, her face swathed in mystery, as she danced toward the guest of honor again, staring into the deep hazel eyes that had never left her. She felt drawn to him like a magnet. Suddenly it wasn't just her and the music. It was him. He had invaded her sensual

15

realm, the realm that had always before been hers alone. She was truly dancing for him.

Chuck swallowed as Fatima danced toward him a second time. He clenched his hands into fists, his breathing hard and labored. He watched as she swayed toward him, her scarf waving gracefully in her hands as she whipped it to and fro, swinging it out in the air and then around her body. Slowly, slowly, she came toward him as the haunting music pounded in his ears. Then, as the final note sounded, she whipped the scarf around his neck and drew his face down to hers.

Fatima drew the scarf down quickly, giving the man no time to escape. She didn't understand it, she had never done anything like this before, but she wanted to kiss him, to have his lips on hers and to know the feel of his body against hers. She felt him expel a surprised breath, and then his lips were on hers, warm and firm and moist and tingling. She moved against his mouth, the Scotch he had been drinking lightly flavoring his lips. Without realizing what she was doing, she forced his mouth to open to hers, deepening the kiss to a greater intimacy as she slid her arms around his neck and curled her fingers into the hair at his nape.

Slowly they kissed, and at some point, Fatima was not sure when, the man took over and he was kissing her. His lips moved against hers, sweeping her lips and her tongue with devastating intimacy. One hand crept around her waist and the other rested on her shoulder, anchoring her body next to the hard warmth of his. As passion overcame all reason, Fatima moved even closer to the man, loving the way her breasts were flattened against his chest. Her hands reaching higher, she stroked his cheeks with her palms. She was weak and dizzy with desire for him.

16

Slowly, reluctantly, Fatima withdrew her fingers from his face as he raised his head from hers. Their eyes still locked together, she stepped back and pulled her scarf from around his shoulders, then bowed low at his feet, her hair trailing the floor. She stayed like that for a moment, then leaped to her feet and ran gracefully to the door, every eye in the room on her. She bowed once again at the door and fled into the foyer, hearing the clapping and the cheers as she shut the door behind her.

The lights went on and she moved to return for her usual ovation, but as she put her hand on the door she hesitated, reluctant to go back to the now well-lighted room and face the man she had just kissed so passionately. Hearing Ray call her name, she started to push the door open, then shook her head and opened the front door. It would be better not to go back, she decided, wanting the man she had just kissed with all her being to remain a mystery.

Chuck blinked when the lights went back on, but he did not clap and cheer with the rest of the men. He stared at the closing door with a bemused expression, his eyes still hooded with desire. The men clapped and Ray called out for Fatima to come back, but the door did not open. A moment later one of the men by the door said that he thought she was gone. Who was she? Chuck wondered. Who was this Fatima who had just kissed him as he had never been kissed before?

Suddenly Chuck realized that his friends were crowding around him, laughing and teasing. "Boy, she hung one on you!" Danny crowed as he slapped Chuck on the back.

"Yeah, does she kiss like she dances?" Robert teased.

"Chuck, old boy, I never realized you had it in you," another voice called out.

Chuck's face flamed. He had never felt so ridiculous in all his life, he thought: he'd just shared the most passionate kiss of his entire life in front of a room full of his old frat brothers.

The razzing continued for a few minutes, then the men resumed the dirty-joke contest. Chuck edged his way across the room to Ray, hoping to find out who the woman was. He was sure that Ray would know.

Ray greeted him with a huge grin. "Who was she?" Chuck asked, hoping his voice remained calm.

Ray shrugged. "Like I said before, I just know her as Fatima." He picked up a cake knife and handed it to Chuck.

Since most of the guests were more interested in telling dirty jokes than in singing "Happy Birthday," Chuck cut himself and Ray a piece of cake and sat down on the couch.

"No, I mean it, Ray! Who is she? Do you have her phone number?"

"I threw it away. I didn't think I'd need it again," Ray replied, thinking to himself that he was becoming an accomplished liar in his old age and hoping that his sneaky scheming would work out. "Hot little number, wasn't she? Wish to God it had been my birthday!"

Chuck nodded, his desire to find out more about Fatima gone. He was the guest of honor, and that kiss had probably been part of her act. She had probably been able to tell by looking at him that he would be a little embarrassed by something like that, he thought, and had done it to tease him. Oh, well, buddy, you should have known, he told himself as he bit into the overly sweet, sticky cake. You couldn't rouse that kind of passion if you had to! Sighing, he ate the cake and finished off another drink, but still had Fatima's fiery kiss on his mind two hours later as he pulled off his clothes and climbed into his big, lonely bed.

Faye Catalini unlocked the door to her luxurious condominium, stepped inside, locked the door behind her, and switched on the light. The sunken living room was bathed in a soft glow and Faye sank into the velvet sofa and snuggled down into the fluffy cushions. She stretched her shoulders like a cat, the silky scarves of her dancing costume shimmering in the lamplight. She had enjoyed dancing for the party tonight— No, she thought, tonight had been *more* than simple enjoyment. She had wanted to dance for the party tonight, needed it even. It had been so long since she'd been able to let herself go like that and move her body with the music.

Faye crossed her arms over her chest and stared up at the ceiling as she breathed in and out slowly. She knew she would have to go to bed soon, since tomorrow was a workday. Tonight had been fun, she thought—it had afforded her the opportunity to express herself in a way that she could never do at her regular job.

Faye stood up and headed toward the kitchen, the coins at her hips jangling but her dancing slippers making no sound on the kitchen tiles. "Hey, Lenore, did Mama go off and forget to feed you?" she asked in her soft, sexy voice as a dainty little Siamese curled herself around Faye's legs.

The cat purred deeply in her throat as Faye bent down and got a packet of cat food from under the kitchen sink. "Here you go, angel," she said as she poured the food into the cat's container.

Then Faye pulled a bottle of wine out of the refrigerator.

Bad habit, she thought as she poured herself a generous glass, bringing it with her to the bedroom. But she was a little keyed up, she thought, as always after dancing, and the wine would help her relax. She needed to sleep well if she was going to make a good impression tomorrow when she reported for her first day on the job with the new accounting firm.

She stared at herself in the mirror, looking into the dark, smoky eyes of the exotic woman who stared back at her. Hair billowing wildly around her head and down her back, eyes deeply ringed and shadowed, makeup heavy and vivid, she was the image of abandoned sensuality. Sometimes she felt as if a stranger were looking back at her in the mirror when she had on her dancing costume. But not tonight. Tonight she felt at one with the woman she had named "Fatima." It was a shame that she had to get out of her costume and put Fatima away for the evening, Faye thought. But she would be dancing again soon, she told herself, and Fatima could make another appearance then.

"Well, off you go, Fatima," she said as she carefully unzipped the hip-skimming skirt and stepped out of it, cautious not to step on any of the billowing layers of skirts. Next came the top. Faye untucked all her scarves one by one and unhooked the back, letting the top slide forward into her hands and freeing her high, firm breasts. As she laid the two pieces carefully across her wing chair, she thought that it was too bad she wasn't really as busty as she looked in her costume, but at least her breasts were high and firm and only a little small for her full, smooth hips.

She unsnapped her shoes and, clad only in a pair of bikini panties, went into the bathroom. She glanced at herself in the mirror as she reached for a tube of cleansing

20

cream—her stomach supple and her legs long and shapely, kept that way by the demands of dancing. She had an attractive body, and the dancing had given her a grace and sensuality that went beyond mere physical appearance.

As Faye applied cleansing cream to her face and pulled off the fake beauty mark she wore on her temple, she wondered again why Ray had been so insistent that she dance for this particular party, the night before she was to report to Cox and Wilson. She had begun to refuse, but Ray had begged her to dance, assuring her that none of her new associates would be in attendance, and since he had done her the tremendous favor of recommending her for her new position, she felt she couldn't turn him down. Besides, she thought, the look on the birthday boy's face when she danced up to him had been priceless!

Faye wiped her face with a soft washcloth and adjusted the temperature in the shower. She stepped in and turned her face to the spray, the feel of the water reminding her of the touch of the birthday boy's lips on hers. She reached up and stroked her lips lightly with her fingers. She had given in to a sudden impulse and kissed a stranger to whom she felt inexplicably drawn. Although the man wasn't her usual type, she had felt a surge of attraction so strong that, when woven into the already sensual atmosphere of her dance, she had been unable to resist. She had kissed him, she thought, with all the sensuality she possessed, and when he'd gotten over his shock he had kissed her back as thoroughly, leaving her wanting more.

Faye shook out her long hair and let the water run through it, telling herself to forget the kiss from the good-looking stranger, that in all probability she would never see him again. He probably thinks I kiss all the men I dance for, she thought as she took a hand-held nozzle and aimed it into the mass of wet hair. The tightly sprayed curls melted into long straight hair and the glitter she had sprayed into the tangled tresses ran out and into a puddle on the bottom of her shower stall.

If the man had thought anything about the kiss at all, she mused, he must have thought it part of the act. Besides, it had probably embarrassed him: Although he'd appeared good-looking in the flickering candlelight, he had a buttoned-down, no-nonsense look. It was the same buttoned-down, no-nonsense look, Faye thought, that she had to adopt so much of the time. If his appearance had been anything to go by, he wasn't the type of man to kiss a belly dancer in front of a whole roomful of men.

But on the other hand, who would think that Faye Catalini, the new tax manager for Cox and Wilson, had a secret life as Fatima the belly dancer? Faye smiled as she squirted shampoo into her long tresses and worked out the rest of the glitter. Yes, she had a secret.

By day she was a talented accountant who had made a meteoric rise from the "pit"—the starting place for all young accountants—to the position of manager in eight short years, during which she had also earned her Master's degree in accounting. If all went well, she thought, in ten years she would become a partner in a large Houston firm.

But by night she was Fatima, and although Faye certainly didn't need the money, she danced professionally once or twice each week, except during tax season, and taught a class in exotic dancing once a week. The dancing expressed another side of her personality—a sensual, highly creative, and demonstrative side that had no place in the business world. Although she was a good accountant and enjoyed her work, accounting alone wasn't enough.

Faye rinsed the shampoo from her hair and stepped from the shower, toweling her hair and her body quickly and stepping into a lacy blue teddy. She sipped the cool wine that waited for her on her dresser and stared into the face in the mirror.

Who would guess that the elegant face that stared back at her had belonged to Fatima just a few minutes ago? she wondered. Very few people, she thought, which was fortunate. If the fact that she was Fatima was ever to become public knowledge in the conservative world of accounting, her accounting career would be severely damaged, if not totally ruined. But since she used another name when she danced, and her appearance was so radically different, she was able to juggle both careers, and had even danced on an occasion or two when someone she knew as Faye Catalini had seen her and not recognized her as Fatima.

Faye pulled back the sheets and slid into bed, leaning against the pillows to sip her wine. Yes, she had juggled both careers for quite a while now and had never been caught, but her dual existence had not been without problems, particularly concerning men. Since it was imperative that Fatima remain a secret in the world of accounting, Faye had never become close to any of the people she met at work, nor dated any of the men she met there.

She was only close to a few old friends like Carol and Ray Donovan, people she could trust with her secret. Besides, even if she were able to be honest about Fatima with her conservative colleagues, she thought, would any of the men she met in the accounting world have understood the mysterious and sensual side of her nature? Faye thought not, and since she agreed with Ray Donovan that most accountants were crashing bores anyway, she didn't date her colleagues, or even socialize with them much.

Faye sighed and sipped her wine. *I'll bet not a man at that party tonight thought Fatima would be going to bed alone,* she thought as she looked around at her beautifully decorated, lonely bedroom. Every one of them probably thought Fatima had a line of men waiting outside her door! And she probably could have, she thought, if she had chosen to live up to her image as Fatima, the sensuous belly dancer.

She met a lot of men as Fatima, and knew she could have had them in the palm of her hand because of the power of her sensual dancing. Yet those men had a preconceived notion of what Fatima was, and Faye had grown tired of the heated words and anger when a man found out that Faye wasn't promiscuous. So she contented herself with the company of her friends and her cat and her dancing.

Faye stretched her long legs and sighed with fatigue. Her kind of dancing took a lot out of her. And she would be even more tired, she thought, come summer, when she'd dance two or three times a week. If there was a drawback to her lifestyle, she thought, it wasn't the loneliness or the secrecy. It was the demanding pace of juggling two jobs, two lives. Accounting demanded fifty hours a week, and the dancing at least two evenings on top of that, and sometimes even more.

Faye set her empty wineglass on the nightstand and turned out the light. *I hope this job works out tomorrow,* she thought as she stared into the darkness. *I'd like to be a partner in that firm someday.*

Ray had said that Charles Goodall, the audit manager she'd be working with, was one of the best accountants he knew. As she snuggled down beneath the soft covers, she pictured a nice old-grandfather type who would show her pictures of his grandchildren. A wicked smile played across her lips as she thought of the proper old gentleman she would meet tomorrow. Wouldn't he be shocked if he knew that his businesslike colleague was also Fatima!

CHAPTER TWO

Faye took a deep breath and pushed open the thick outer door that read COX AND WILSON, her poised appearance masking the nervousness and excitement that she felt as she strode confidently up to the round desk where the company receptionist was talking softly into the telephone.

Faye didn't doubt her ability to handle the position of manager; she had held a similar position for six months in her old firm. But Cox and Wilson was a much larger firm, one of the biggest nationally. Her job here would involve working closely with other accountants, something she hadn't done too much of before, and she hoped her new colleagues would be easy to work with.

Faye waited patiently for the receptionist to finish her conversation, meanwhile glancing down at her rust-colored silk suit and the light cream blouse with the big bow at her neck that she'd chosen to wear on her first day. She had decided to wait until tomorrow to wear one of the expensive silk dresses that she preferred.

Faye disliked the "dress for success" fashions of many of her female colleagues, considering it bland. But she realized the importance of dressing appropriately for the office. Today she'd pinned her hair back into a soft businesslike knot and wore muted makeup that nevertheless managed to accent her considerable beauty. Her only jewelry was a simple watch and a pair of gold hoop earrings. As a result she blended in perfectly with the businesslike atmosphere of the office she was standing in, and wondered what the reaction would have been if she'd walked in here as Fatima.

The young receptionist spoke softly into the mouthpiece, punched one of the buttons on the telephone console in front of her, then looked up at Faye. "I'm sorry to keep you waiting," she said as she hung up the telephone. "That was one of our more troublesome clients. May I help you?"

"I'm Faye Catalini, the new tax manager," Faye said as she extended her hand.

"Oh, Miss Catalini, I'm so glad to meet you!" the young woman replied, her blond curls bouncing around her plump face. "When I heard we were getting a lady tax manager, I could hardly wait for you to get here."

"Thank you," Faye said, puzzled.

"You see, I want to be an accountant myself in a few years," the receptionist explained. "And if you're here in the office, maybe I can learn from you."

Faye smiled warmly at her. "The first thing you better do is tell me your name," she suggested.

"Oh. I'm Darlin," she said.

Faye's mouth dropped open at the girl's pronouncement. "Uh, I'm sure you are, but what's your name?"

The girl laughed. "That's it. I'm Darlin Jackson. My mama said that my daddy took one look at me the night I was born and declared I was the most darlin' little thing he'd ever seen, and it stuck. They even put it on my birth certificate. Anyway, Mr. Wilson said to bring you back to his office as soon as you got here." She stood up and motioned for Faye to come with her.

Faye couldn't help smiling to herself at the enthusiastic young woman as Darlin chattered in her ear all the way down the long corridor. Darlin was very carefully dressed in a prim gray suit and white blouse, but the businesslike effect was completely destroyed by the rioting blond curls that cascaded down her back and the glamorous makeup she'd applied. Faye sighed with relief: Cox and Wilson couldn't be too stuffy if they kept Darlin!

Darlin knocked softly on a door at the end of the hall, then opened it and stuck her head in the door. "Mr. Wilson, Miss Catalini's here."

"That's good, send her in," Mr. Wilson said as Darlin threw open the door. Faye stepped inside and pulled the door shut behind her. "Good morning, Faye, it's good to see you again," he said, moving from behind his desk as Faye strode across the room and extended her hand.

"Good morning, Mr. Wilson," she said to him, recalling his lack of distinguishing features as they shook hands. It seemed to her, in fact, that he was bland to the point of blending into the woodwork. But his reputation was imposing, even if his physical characteristics were not, and Faye considered herself lucky to be in his employ. "I'm so glad to be here today."

"And we're fortunate to have you," Mr. Wilson returned graciously. "Would you care for a cup of coffee?"

"Yes, thank you, I would," Faye replied as Mr. Wilson opened an accordion door and revealed a cabinet and a coffeemaker. He poured her a cup, and when Faye said she took it black, handed it to her. Faye sipped the coffee and murmured, "Umm, delicious."

"Darlin makes it for me," he said.

"She makes delicious coffee," Faye said, wondering again how such a flamboyant receptionist had managed to

28

stay on at such a stuffy firm. Maybe receptionists weren't expected to be as proper as the accountants were, she thought.

They sat down and talked for a few minutes while drinking their coffee. Mr. Wilson used the time to briefly review with Faye what her new responsibilities would be. As tax manager she would be responsible for very little of the actual accounting and figuring drudgery—the beginners in the pit, he said, the kids fresh out of college, would do that. She would be supervising those accountants and the senior accountant managing the pit; she would also do more of the actual tax planning, and have a great deal of client contact.

Mr. Wilson made a point to mention Radbury Oil, one of the firm's biggest clients and one of the firms Faye would be responsible for. "As I told you, you'll be working a lot with Charles Goodall on Radbury Oil," he said. "He's the manager of the audit department, and one of the best accountants I've ever worked with. Ray Donovan recommended him two years ago and I've been grateful ever since." He drained his coffee cup and set it on his desk.

"Maybe Ray just likes to work with his friends," Faye teased as she put her empty coffee cup on the desk too.

Mr. Wilson shook his head. "Ray's got a talent for spotting talent in other accountants. That's one of the reasons I hired you. Ray always picks a winner."

Faye gulped back a sudden wave of apprehension. "I'll do my best to live up to your expectations," she said as she and Mr. Wilson both stood.

They walked to the door together, Mr. Wilson opening it for her. "Let me introduce you around," he said, "and then I'll show you to your office."

He escorted her back down the hall and into a large

29

room where five accountants were working. "This is the pit you'll be supervising," he said, then introduced her to each of the accountants.

The young men's eyes widened a little at the sight of their young and pretty boss, but they did not verbally express their surprise. They're playing the role well, Faye thought as she followed Mr. Wilson out of the pit: Cookie-cutter conservative, every one of them. When she'd met Darlin she had thought that maybe, just maybe, Cox and Wilson was going to be different, less stuffy than other accounting firms, but the inhabitants of the pit had proven her wrong. The senior supervisor, Warden Smith, greeted her politely but was reserved, and Faye wondered if he had been disappointed about not getting her position.

"There's one more person I want you to meet before I show you to your new office," Mr. Wilson said as he knocked on another door. "I'd like to introduce you to Chuck Goodall, our audit manager. As I said before, you'll be working with him a lot in the next few months."

A masculine voice called out to them to enter, and Faye fixed a friendly smile on her face as she prepared to meet the grandfatherly audit manager she had pictured last night. She followed Mr. Wilson into the spacious office and closed the door behind her, then as she turned around and got her first look at Charles Goodall, froze in her tracks. *Ohmygod,* she thought as her eyes widened at the sight of the tall, brown-haired accountant in horn-rimmed glasses, carefully dressed in a pinstripe suit and a matching blue tie. He was the birthday boy! He was the man she had danced for and then kissed so passionately last night! What was she going to do now? she wondered.

Faye shook her head slightly while following Mr. Wilson into the room, her eyes never leaving Charles Goodall's handsome face. It was him, it had to be him. Even though the lights were dim last night, she had seen his face and those big hazel eyes behind the thick glasses. *Ray Donovan, I'm going to kill you for this!* she thought as she waited for recognition to dawn in Charles Goodall's eyes. She knew that Ray loved a practical joke, but this had gone too far! Her career could go down the drain if Charles did not have a sense of humor, she thought.

Unaware of the fear and apprehension that gripped Faye, Mr. Wilson motioned her forward. Charles extended his hand, warmth and friendliness in his face. "I'm so glad to meet you," he said quietly. "Ray has said so many nice things about the work you do."

I'll just bet he has! Faye thought to herself as she wondered just which job Ray had been referring to. She briefly considered boiling Ray in hot oil but decided that would be too humane. "Thank you," she said equally softly, staring up into his hazel eyes, waiting for him to recognize her and dreading that moment. Or was he just playing with her? she wondered. Did he already know who she was? Were he and Ray having a laugh at her expense? Well, if that was the case, she decided, she would go along with the charade.

"I'm glad to meet you, too," she said as she shook his hand. "I've heard a lot of nice things about your work also." She watched his face closely, looking for some sign of amusement or sarcasm, but found only quiet friendliness.

"Well, I just wanted to make sure you two met before I showed Faye to her new office," Mr. Wilson said as he motioned for Faye to accompany him. "Would you like to see where you will be spending your time?"

"Faye, would you mind if I came by your office about

ten-thirty?" Charles Goodall asked as Faye followed Mr. Wilson out the door. "I would like to go over the Radbury Oil account with you. We're doing an audit right now and we'll be needing your input within the next few days."

"Certainly," Faye replied before shutting the door behind her. Had he recognized her? she asked herself again. Did he know who she was? *Ray, you rat, how could you set me up like that?* she wailed inwardly as she followed Mr. Wilson down the hall and through the door marked FAYE CATALINI.

Her eyes lit up, Charles Goodall temporarily forgotten, as she looked around at the spacious, comfortable office where she would be spending much of her time. Although it was smaller than Mr. Wilson's, it was the same size as Charles's, and had two comfortable wing chairs as well as her desk chair. She pulled the drapes behind the desk and stared out the window at the view of downtown Houston, people and traffic bustling in the late April sunshine.

"This is lovely, Mr. Wilson," she said as she drew the drapes and shut out the glaring sunlight.

"We want you to be comfortable. Here are a few of our major accounts. I thought you might like to look them over," he said as he motioned to a huge pile of documents piled in the middle of the desk. "You will need to become very familiar with them. I'll leave you alone now. Would you like Darlin to bring you another cup of coffee?"

Faye nodded and sat down at her desk. It was homework time! she told herself as Mr. Wilson left the room. Thank goodness she didn't have another dancing job until the weekend—it would take her that long to wade through all these papers.

It occurred to her that if Charles Goodall recognized her and said something to Mr. Wilson about her performance the previous night, she'd be through almost as soon as she'd begun. How could Ray have arranged something that stupid? she thought, then pushed aside the disturbing thought in order to begin working.

Faye picked up the first document in the pile, the financial records of a large ranch, and looked it over carefully while sipping the coffee that Darlin placed at her elbow. As always, she lost herself completely in the facts and figures in front of her. She made her way through the ranch records and was halfway through a folder on a medium-sized real estate firm when Charles Goodall knocked softly on her door. Receiving no response, he opened her door a crack and peered inside at the beautiful woman whose head was bent over a bulky folder.

"Faye?" he called softly from the door.

Faye jumped and put down the folder. "C-come in," she stammered as she stood up to meet him. He strode into the room and shut the door behind him, then plopped a couple of folders onto her desk and sat down in one of the chairs beside her desk. "The Radbury account?" she asked, gesturing to the folders.

Charles nodded as she sat down across from him and handed her the first folder. "That's last year's overall statement of the Radbury Oil Company. You'll find statements for the last five years in there, and the tax returns."

Faye nodded and looked over the statements while Chuck continued to fill her in on the work his department had done with Radbury Oil. Though she heard what he was saying, a part of her was reliving last night's passionate embrace. He certainly didn't act as though he knew who she was, she thought. He was friendly enough, but he wasn't treating her with any degree of familiarity, nor had he made any kind of innuendo that would indicate that he knew her secret.

Faye studied him through lowered lashes as he continued to fill her in on the oil company. He was tall and slim without being too skinny, and his tailored suit looked as though it might be concealing a hard, fit body. His face was handsome, almost boyish behind the thick horn-rimmed glasses that he occasionally had to push back up on his nose. Now who did he remind her of? she wondered. Of course! Clark Kent, Superman's alter ego.

As the morning wore on and Chuck continued to work with her, Faye realized that he had a dry, gentle wit behind the shy exterior. With just a word or two, he made her chuckle. His low-key charm appealed to her more than the more common macho ideal. His attractiveness grew on Faye until, by the end of the morning, she was astonished by just how drawn she was to him. He wasn't her usual type, that was for sure! she thought.

Chuck leaned back in his chair and tried not to stare at the lovely woman who sat across from him. So this was the famous Faye Catalini! No wonder her reputation had preceded her, he thought. Not only was she stunningly attractive, if her questions and comments were anything to go by, she was also a fantastic accountant. Chuck glanced admiringly across at her firm, womanly figure. Not too busty, he thought. I like that. He let his gaze roam upward, past her suit-concealed figure to her aristocratic facial features. Have I ever met her before? he asked himself. She seemed familiar, yet he was sure that if he'd met her he certainly wouldn't have forgotten it.

It was nearly noon when Faye laid aside the thick folder that had been in her lap. "I don't think my mind can absorb any more of this right now," she admitted as she stood up and stretched the kinks out of her muscles. Chuck stared at the unconsciously provocative movement and swallowed. "I'll go over the rest of the material tonight when I go over these other files," she added.

"Uh, that will be fine," Chuck said as he stood up and opened his mouth to speak. But just as he was forming the words to invite Faye out to lunch, the door to Faye's office flew open and Ray Donovan stuck his head through the door.

Chuck and Faye both turned their heads toward the open door. "Ray!" they both said in unison, then Chuck turned around to Faye in surprise.

"I didn't know you knew Ray," he said.

"Yes, I know Faye," Ray said as his eyes leaped back and forth from one of them to the other. "You've never met her before?"

Cute, Ray. I'm going to skewer you over a bed of hot coals, Faye thought as irrepressible mirth shone out of Ray's eyes.

Chuck shook his head slowly from side to side. "No, Faye and I have never met," he said.

Ray shot a glance at Faye, who was shooting daggers at him out of her eyes. "Are you sure?" he pressed.

"Positive," Faye broke in quickly.

"If I had met Faye before, I'm sure I would have remembered her," Chuck added gallantly.

Chuck turned his back to put a folder on Faye's desk and Ray used the opportunity to wink broadly at Faye. She glowered at him, but he just grinned and shrugged his shoulders. Chuck turned around suddenly and Faye quickly rearranged her face into a bland smile that she hoped would fool Chuck.

"Ray," he said, "I was just about to ask Faye to join me

35

for lunch. Would you like to come with us? I'm sure you and Faye have a lot to talk about."

Faye opened her mouth to protest, but Ray took her by the arm and started with her toward the door. "You bet, Chuck. Faye and I have a lot of catching up to do. It's been *so long* since I've seen her!" He escorted a sputtering Faye out the door, leaving Chuck to follow them.

"I need to stop by my desk and make a quick phone call, then I'll be right with you," Chuck said, and ducked into his office.

Faye waited until the door was shut then wrenched her arm out from under Ray's and whirled on him angrily. "What do you mean by setting me up like that? Having me dance for a man I have to work with, for goodness sake! Are you trying to wreck my career?" she hissed in a loud whisper.

Ray had the audacity to laugh out loud at her anger. "I'm not the one who chose to hang a big smooch on him, you were," he teased, his eyes dancing. "Besides, he didn't recognize you, did he?"

"But what if he had?" Faye cried, then lowered her voice when she realized just how loud she had been. "What if he had known who I was this morning? It could have been the end of my accounting career. Ray, I know you like a practical joke, but this time you went too far!"

Ray shook his head. "You're way too uptight about keeping your dancing a secret," he declared. "So what if Chuck had recognized you? He wouldn't have run to old man Wilson with it."

"How do you know— Oh, Chuck, are you finished with your call?" she asked sweetly as Chuck emerged from his office and shut the door behind him.

Chuck looked from Faye to Ray, wondering why Faye

36

was swelled up like a porcupine and Ray was grinning like a Cheshire cat, but Faye quickly tucked her arm in his and headed with him toward the door, leaving Ray to trail behind them.

They rode the elevator down in silence and left the office building, stepping out into the hot Houston sunlight. "So where to?" Faye asked as she looked from Ray to Chuck.

"Do you have a favorite?" Chuck asked.

"Not in the downtown area," she said. "My last office was out close to the Galleria."

"How about that little place we tried last week?" Ray asked. "It was pretty good."

Chuck nodded, and the three of them set off down the street, Faye's heels clicking on the pavement as she hurried to keep up with Chuck's and Ray's longer strides. She looked up at Chuck, then glanced over at Ray, and was infuriated to see a grin on his face. If he tells Chuck, I'll kill him and tell God he died, she thought as she glanced up at Chuck. She had the feeling Chuck was somewhat proper—that he wouldn't find the story funny.

The restaurant Ray had suggested was only a couple of blocks away, and catered to the daytime business world of downtown Houston. A harried waiter seated them and handed them a menu. When he returned to take their order, Faye asked for soup and a cup of coffee, and Ray ordered a small steak. Chuck only ordered a small salad and a glass of iced tea.

"Not hungry?" she asked softly as she handed the waiter her menu.

Chuck shook his head. "Not particularly."

"Well, it's no wonder," Ray piped up. "As much as you ate last night, it's a wonder you want anything at all today."

Chuck grinned at Ray. "You ate just as much," he replied.

"Yeah, but you're not trying to grow one of these," he said as he patted his small potbelly. Ray turned to Faye. "We gave Chuck here a birthday party last night."

"Oh, you did?" she asked, trying to sound casual. "What birthday was it in honor of, if you don't mind my asking?"

"Just like a woman, wants to know all your vital statistics," Ray teased as Faye blushed.

"I don't mind telling. I'm thirty-five," Chuck replied, hoping to ease Faye's embarrassment. "A little older than you are, I guess."

"Five years," she said without batting an eye. "Some of us aren't ashamed to tell our ages," she informed Ray loftily. She turned back to Chuck and smiled. "Was it a nice party?" she asked politely.

"Was it ever!" Ray crowed. "Let me tell you about it!"

Why didn't I keep my mouth shut? Faye thought as a dull red started to creep up Chuck's neck.

"I don't think Faye really wants to hear about our party," Chuck said.

"Oh, sure she does," Ray said as Faye groaned inwardly. "Don't you, Faye?"

"Whatever you say, Ray," she said, considering the effect a small bomb left on the front seat of Ray's car would have.

"Well, Faye, you wouldn't believe it! We thought maybe Chuck needed his tired blood perked up a little, so we called this hot little number to come and dance for him."

"A dancer?" Faye asked.

"Yeah, a belly dancer," Ray continued. "And she shows up with her top cut up to here and her bottom cut down to

38

there"—Ray gestured to about where Fatima's costume was cut—"and she does this dance that you wouldn't *believe.*"

"I don't think Faye wants to hear about the dancer," Chuck said. His face turned even redder as he recalled the way Fatima's body had shimmied and bounced in the darkened living room.

Ray ignored Chuck. "Anyway, that woman must have muscles and nerves the rest of us don't have. She could get her tummy going one way and her bottom going another and her arms all up and going—"

"Really, Ray, don't you think—"

"Just a minute, I'm getting to the good part," Ray said enthusiastically as both Faye and Chuck groaned inwardly, for different reasons. "Anyway, once this gal's finished with her dancing, she takes one of these scarves and wraps it around Chuck here and she kisses the living daylights out of him. Right in front of everybody! Honest to Pete, I think every man in the room would have changed places with Chuck about then. How about it, Chuck? Can the lady kiss as well as she can dance?"

"Really, Ray," Chuck objected, looking over at Faye, who sat with a look of horror on her face. "I think you're embarrassing Faye."

He knows he is! she thought as Ray grinned outrageously.

"Oh, Faye, you should have seen this guy. Don't let him kid you today, he *loved* that dancer! Even asked me about her afterward."

"Wh-what did you tell him?" Faye asked through stiff lips.

"Ray—" Chuck began warningly.

Ray lifted his shoulders in a reluctant shrug. "What

could I tell him? I told him her name was Fatima and that I didn't know any more about her than that."

Faye released the breath she had been holding while Chuck glowered at Ray. "Well, I certainly didn't want to have any more to do with her," Chuck snapped as the waiter put their dishes in front of them. "I was just curious. She's probably just a hooker anyway."

Faye choked on the spoonful of soup she'd been about to swallow. Chuck reached out and patted her back gently until she stopped choking. "I didn't mean to embarrass you, Faye," he said as Faye tried valiantly to swallow her soup.

"Um, that's all right," she said as soon as she had managed to get the soup past her constricted vocal cords. "Tell me, Chuck, will we be working on any other accounts as big as Radbury Oil?" she said quickly, vowing that if Ray said one more word about Fatima, she wasn't going to wait for the bed of coals, she was going to kill him right now with her bare hands, and then she might have a go at Chuck. A hooker indeed!

Ray turned most of his attention to his steak, and Faye and Chuck carried on a conversation that Faye only participated in with half her mind. So he thought Fatima was probably a hooker, she thought. Of all the narrow-mindedness! But really, why was she surprised? Wasn't this exactly why she had kept her dancing a secret in the accounting world? Yes, he probably thought Fatima was a hooker, but then most of his colleagues would have thought the same thing. Disappointment flooded Faye and it was all she could do to keep up the polite social facade and eat her lunch. Chuck Goodall was just as proper on the inside as he was on the outside, she thought, even if he was the most appealing man she had met in a long time. She would never be able to share her secret with him.

Faye ate the rest of her soup and thanked Ray when he volunteered to pick up the tab for the three of them, promising to take the two men out at a later date. Back at the office Chuck and Ray disappeared to tackle the afternoon's work. Faye went into her office, too, and shut the door, but instead of going straight to work, she mused about the passionate kiss she and Chuck had shared the night before. If only she hadn't kissed him like that, she thought, he might have thought the whole thing was funny. But, no, she had overstepped the bounds of the dancing and had singled him out for a passionate display. Why hadn't she left well enough alone? she asked herself. Since she hadn't, she knew she was going to have to be more careful than ever so Chuck would never find out who Fatima was. Faye sighed and uncrossed her legs. I'll just have to make sure he doesn't ever know, she vowed, knowing it was going to be hard, since she'd never been in this much danger of exposure before.

Chuck ran his hand down the back of his neck and sighed in frustration. This was the third time he and his crew had gone in to audit this particular company, and this was the third set of conflicting figures they had come up with. Where were the mistakes coming from? he wondered. Was it in his office or was the company trying to pull a fast one? Swearing softly at the mangled accounts, he pushed up his sleeve and read the dial of his wristwatch. Nearly six. He'd been there since seven-thirty this morning.

Cox and Wilson has had enough of my time today, he decided as he shut the folder and flopped it on his desk. It wasn't tax season and there was no burning rush—he could finish the account in the morning. Standing and stretching, he pulled his coat off the back of his chair, put it on over his broad shoulders, then left his office and shut the door firmly behind him. He wasn't even taking a brief-case of work home with him tonight, he thought.

Chuck headed down the corridor, whistling softly under his breath, then paused when he saw Faye's door slightly ajar. He could see her inside, her head bent over one of the stack of folders on her desk. Old man Wilson didn't believe in easing someone into the job, he thought, that was for sure. Yet he had to admit he agreed with him: If Faye was going to come in and function properly, she had to know each and every account that she was supposed to advise on taxes.

But she did look tired, he thought, sitting with her el-bow resting on the desk and her chin in her hand. Chuck put his hand on the doorknob, then hesitated. He'd wanted to ask her to lunch to get to know her better, then had been embarrassed by Ray's revelations to Faye. As a result he hadn't had a chance to discuss anything but business with her. And he wanted to, he mused, he wanted to very much.

But would she be willing to go out to dinner with him, especially on this short notice? he wondered, sure he wasn't her type. Besides, she probably had a boyfriend. No, he better just let it go, he decided.

Chuck was about to turn around and head for the door when he caught himself up short. *Ask her, chicken,* he thought as his fingers tightened on the doorknob. *This was your problem with women when you were single. You just assumed they would say no. You never gave them a chance to say yes. Goodall, go in there and ask!*

42

Chuck pushed open the door to Faye's office and closed it quietly behind him. "Still at it?" he asked softly.

Faye jumped. "You startled me," she explained as she pushed the folder aside. "Taking an afternoon coffee break?"

"No, I'm going home," Chuck said. "It's almost six."

Faye looked at her watch and gasped. "Good grief, I thought it was about four! I guess I ought to go home myself," she said as she marked her place in the folder.

She packed it into her briefcase along with several other folders on her desk. Chuck swallowed back nervousness as Faye tucked a small purse in with the folders and snapped her briefcase shut. Ask her, he said to himself. Don't let her get away from here.

"Well, I guess that's it," she said.

"Would you like to have dinner with me tonight?" Chuck burst out, then felt his face flame. Good grief, couldn't he have been a little more sophisticated about it? Did he have to blush like a teenager? He watched closely as expressions crossed Faye's face, first surprise and then reluctance, and he felt his own face fall. She's going to say no, he thought. I should have known she wouldn't want to go out with anyone as boring as I am.

Suddenly Faye's face broke into a wide smile. "I can spare a couple of hours. Yes, Chuck, I'd love to go out with you. Can you give me a minute to freshen up in the ladies' room?"

Faye, you have to be crazy, she thought a few minutes later as she stared at her face in the mirror and tried to repair the damage that eleven hours had done to her makeup. You know that you never go out with the men you work with. They're boring, and besides, if you do, you run the risk of being exposed as Fatima. And you don't

want that! With trembling fingers she tucked a stray wisp
of hair back into her chignon and stared at her wide eyes in
the mirror. Chuck Goodall, who already thinks that Fatima is a hooker, is the last man that you have any business
going out with! she told herself. So why did you say yes?

She shrugged her shoulders and applied a fresh coat of
lipstick. It was the look in his eyes that had done it, she
thought. He had been frightened and nervous when he'd
suddenly come out with the invitation, and when her reluctance showed, his face had fallen and his eyes had
looked like those of a whipped puppy. He was painfully
shy yet had worked up the courage to ask her out. She
hadn't had the heart to say no. But Faye had to admit that
she'd accepted for another reason too: Spending the evening with this quiet, humorous man sounded like heaven
to her. But what if they hit it off and he wanted to take her
out again? she wondered. What about Chuck and Fatima?
I'll deal with that later, she told herself firmly as she
dusted her nose with a little powder and straightened her
shoulders.

"Ready?" Chuck asked as Faye emerged from the ladies'
room, her face fresh and her hair straightened.

Faye nodded.

"Have any preferences?" he asked.

"Anywhere without Ray," Faye suggested dryly.

"That sounds fair," Chuck replied. "Listen, I have my
car here and so do you, so why don't we meet at that new
Chinese restaurant out on Westheimer?"

To Faye's delight, he'd referred to a new restaurant that
she'd been dying to try but simply had not had time to visit
yet. "Sounds great," she said as they left the office together.

Faye shivered in the gloomy underground garage, deserted except for her and Chuck. "This place gives me the creeps," she admitted as she grimaced.

"That's understandable," Chuck said as they walked toward her car. "It always makes me just that much more anxious to get out of here. Tell you what. I'll walk you to your car any time you like, even if I'm not ready to go," Chuck volunteered as Faye got out her keys. "See you in a few minutes." He shut the door of her car before Faye even had a chance to thank him for his offer.

Faye followed Chuck's brown Oldsmobile out of the parking lot. Half an hour later they had fought their way through the thick rush-hour traffic and were pulling into the parking lot of the elegant new Chinese restaurant. They entered together and a comely Oriental waitress showed them to their table and handed them menus. Faye suppressed a smile at the admiration in the waitress's eyes as she looked at Chuck, admiration to which he was totally immune. Why, he doesn't even realize that the girl is drooling all over him! she thought with astonishment. He has no idea of his own appeal. Or was he just modest? she wondered, watching him push the thick glasses back up the bridge of his nose and open the menu. No, she decided a moment later, he has no idea that he's so appealing.

They decided to order a dinner for two and had a lively debate over what to order. When the waitress had taken the order and gone, Chuck patted his flat stomach and laughed. "That's going to be a few extra miles in the morning," he said.

"I know what you mean," Faye agreed. She had fought the pounds a little harder for the last year or so. "But it will be worth it. Do you run every morning?"

Chuck nodded. "Anywhere from three to five miles," he said. "How about joining me some morning?"

"Me? Get up out of a nice warm bed and *run?* You have to be out of your mind!" She made a face and Chuck laughed.

Chuck glanced down her long shapely body and raised his eyebrows. "You must do something to keep in shape. What do you do?"

"I da—do calisthenics," Faye said, catching herself in time. She'd nearly admitted that she practiced her dancing an hour or more in the morning before she went to work.

"Exercises? Doesn't that get boring?" Chuck asked, staring at the sleek, supple woman sitting in front of him. He didn't think she was the type that would like calisthenics.

"No more than running does," she said as the waiter put a plate of miniature egg rolls in front of them. Faye picked one up and blew on it until she was convinced it was cool enough, then popped it into her mouth. "Umm, this is delicious," she said, rolling her eyes.

"Yes, it is," Chuck agreed a moment later, as he finished one. He looked across the table at her with curiosity. "I didn't realize until lunchtime that you knew Ray. How long have you known him?"

Too long, Faye thought. "Quite a while," she said. "His wife, Carol, and I were sorority sisters in college."

"You're from up north?" Chuck asked.

"My parents are from New Jersey, but I grew up an Army brat, hence the lack of a regional accent. Carol and I were in college together when she and Ray met. He was in the service at the time. We kept in touch and they kept begging me to move down to Houston, so several years ago, after my parents were killed in a car accident, I did just that and Ray recommended me for my first job here."

Faye laughed. "Ray has a talent for recommending people for jobs."

"I know," Chuck agreed. "He recommended me for this job with Cox and Wilson. We were fraternity brothers and we stayed in touch after graduation. He was my best man, in fact."

Faye's eyes widened and without meaning to she glanced down at his left hand. "I'm divorced," Chuck said tersely.

"I'm sorry," Faye said as her face turned scarlet. "It's just that—"

"You don't have to explain," Chuck said gently. "There are a lot of cheaters out there."

Faye picked up another egg roll and munched on it. "Is the divorce recent?" she asked.

Chuck nodded. "We finalized it about three months ago," he said, then his face split into a grin. "Do you know that this is the first date I've been on in over ten years? Tell me, have dates changed that much?"

Faye shook her head. "I don't think so," she said, her face deadpan. "Tell me, do you have the hands of an octopus, the breath of a hungover elephant, and the enthusiasm of a wet beagle?"

Chuck nodded and laughed out loud. "Yes, yes, yes! I have all those qualities!"

"Then you should do fine," Faye assured him as the waiter set covered dishes in front of them. Faye cautiously lifted the lid of one of the dishes and put some of the moo goo gai pan onto her plate. "Oh, this smells delicious," she enthused.

They quickly filled their plates, and the waiter whisked the serving pieces off the table. Chuck glanced down at Faye's bare left hand. "You've never married?" he asked.

Faye shook her head. " 'Fraid not," she said. "Carol's

47

about to give up on me." She cut a bite of egg foo yung and popped it into her mouth.

"So tell me about yourself."

Carefully censoring her tale to avoid any mention of dancing, Faye talked about growing up in a large Italian family that moved all over the world, about going to third and fourth grade in Panama and two years of high school in Germany; about college in Massachusetts, her first accounting jobs in New York, and her move to Houston five years earlier; and about her sisters and brother scattered all over the country.

Chuck, in turn, told her about growing up in a small town in central Texas the only child of the local banker, about his college years at the University of Texas and his rise in the accounting world. He mentioned being married at twenty-four but said little about his breakup ten years later, and Faye couldn't help but wonder what had happened to sever the marriage.

They laughed and talked long after the food was gone. It was only when Faye happened to glance down at her watch that she realized it was after nine. "Oh, I didn't realize it was so late," she said as Chuck glanced down at his own watch and grimaced. "And I still have two hours' worth of work!"

"Then I'll send you on your way and let you get to it," Chuck said, smiling at her as he pulled out his wallet. After paying, he took Faye by the arm and escorted her through the restaurant. The touch of his hand on her arm was curiously warm and exciting, and Faye longed to touch him as intimately as Fatima had the night before.

Chuck walked her to her car and waited for her to unlock it. "I enjoyed tonight, Faye," he said as he put his arm around her shoulders. "We'll have to do it again."

48

"I'd like that," Faye agreed. Chuck's arm drew her closer to him, and Faye could feel her heart pound. He's going to kiss me and I'm going to give myself away, she thought as Chuck drew her closer. But I don't care, she told herself—I just want to kiss him again.

But this time Chuck pecked her lips lightly, then released her from his grasp. "See you tomorrow," he said as he opened the door of Faye's car for her.

"Uh, sure, Chuck," she said as she got in and Chuck closed the door behind her.

What kind of a kiss was that? she asked herself, disappointed as she drove home through the dark streets. I've gotten better from my brother! Faye wistfully recalled the other kiss and recalled that Chuck hadn't been the one to initiate that one. But he'd kissed her back last night, she thought, so he knew how! Oh, well, maybe he thought Faye wouldn't appreciate it the way Fatima would, she thought, suddenly jealous of her alter ego.

Once he got home, Chuck sat on the couch staring at the rerun of "Charlie's Angels" with unseeing eyes. None of them are half as pretty as Faye, he thought as he watched the three nubile beauties battle whatever bad guy they were battling—Chuck wasn't paying much attention. And she's smarter than they are, too, he thought as one of them made a stupid mistake and got caught. Faye would have known better than to fall for that old trick!

Laughing at his thoughts, Chuck rubbed his eyes and swallowed the last of his beer. Yes, Faye was smart and she was beautiful and she was a lady. She had been embarrassed by Ray's cracks about Fatima and the kind of dance the woman had performed. I'd like to get to know her better, Chuck thought as he walked barefoot to the bathroom and stripped and showered. After putting on a pair of pajama bottoms, he climbed into bed and pulled the covers up to his chin.

But as he closed his eyes, it wasn't the prim and proper Faye Catalini who invaded his thoughts. It was Fatima, the shadowy figure who had danced so alluringly for him and who had kissed him as no other woman had ever kissed him. She had been beautiful, she had been sensual, she had been provocative. And for a brief moment in time she had been his. Chuck groaned and buried his face in the pillow, but for the life of him he couldn't get Fatima and the kiss she had given him off his mind.

CHAPTER THREE

Faye held the telephone to her ear and tried not to laugh out loud. "Yes, Mr. Warner. Now let me see if I understand you correctly. You say that this morning you settled that lawsuit over the oil rights with your old partner." She paused as she listened to the excited voice on the other end of the line. "Yes, I'm sure you're thrilled, I would be too. That's a very generous settlement."

Faye sat quietly, but in the privacy of her office her eyes were dancing with amusement. "No, Mr. Warner, we can't go back and change your returns for the last ten years." She listened and rolled her eyes toward the ceiling. "Yes, sir, I know that the suit's been unsettled all this time." More listening, during which Faye kicked off her shoes and rubbed one foot against the other. "Well, the law simply doesn't allow us to do that. Yes, I know it doesn't seem fair, but that's the law, and we'll get into big trouble if we violate it."

Faye propped her feet up on her desk and wiggled her toes. "What we can do, Mr. Warner, is what is known as income averaging." As she explained the process to him, she picked up the telephone cord in her toes and twirled it around her foot. "No, I don't recommend trying to figure it yourself, but I'd be glad to do it for you. Just bring in all your records and I'll do my best. Yes, the best to you too. Good-bye, Mr. Warner."

Faye leaned forward to hang up the telephone and caught a glimpse of her office door opening. She tried to slide her feet off the desk and hang up the telephone at the same time, but her feet were still tangled in the telephone cord and she jerked the telephone off the desk and onto the top of her feet, stinging them and jangling the bell of the phone. "Oow!" she complained, temporarily forgetting she wasn't alone.

"Faye, are you all right?" Chuck asked anxiously as he rushed into the room and over to her. "What did you do to yourself?"

Faye blushed, embarrassed to be caught in a less than businesslike position. "I pulled the telephone over on my feet," she admitted as she bent down to move the telephone and found the cord badly tangled around her feet and legs. "Oh, I'm tangled up down here," she mumbled as she picked up the phone and tried to unwind the cord.

Chuck rushed around the desk and looked down at the cord wrapped around her feet. "How on earth did you manage that?" he asked as he knelt and took the telephone from her.

"Uh, it wasn't easy," Faye admitted as she remembered playing with the cord with her toes. "How am I going to get out of this?"

Chuck moved the telephone around her legs, blushing furiously as he stared at the long, shapely length of leg that was exposed below her skirt.

"Thank you," Faye said as she beamed her warmest smile at Chuck, who smiled sheepishly at her and began to untangle the cord. He's so nice, she told herself as she imagined the kind of response she would have gotten from many other men.

"That's all right, I'm glad to know you're human," Chuck admitted as he quickly untangled the cord and set the phone back on her desk. "Why, you even have toes!" Faye laughed out loud and Chuck grinned. "I mean, you're so good at your work I was beginning to think you were perfect. How did you manage to get that tangled, anyway?"

"I was on the phone to Ted Warner and I was so bored I played with the cord," Faye admitted, knowing that she wasn't doing her accountant image any good right now but not particularly caring.

"With your *toes?*" Chuck teased.

"You would have played with your toes, too, if you'd had to answer his silly questions," Faye said, and laughed. "He just won a settlement today and he wanted to go back and change his returns for the last ten years! Can you believe that?"

Chuck laughed out loud and handed Faye a folder. "Here are those figures you wanted on Radbury Oil. He's got a lot of exploration and drilling expenses on here from the first quarter."

Faye flipped open the folder and nodded her head. "I'll get to it first thing in the morning," she promised.

"Thanks, I'd appreciate that," Chuck replied. "Say, would you like to go out for dinner tomorrow night?"

Faye mentally reviewed her dancing schedule. She was supposed to dance tonight and Saturday, but Friday night was free. "Sure, I'd love to go out with you," she said.

"Great! We'll decide tomorrow where we'd like to go," Chuck said as he started out of the office. "Now, remember, my number is little-toe, little-toe, middle-toe—" He laughed and ducked out of Faye's office when she stuck her tongue out at him.

I didn't know they made men like him anymore, Faye thought as she watched the door close. She opened the Radbury Oil account and stared at it unseeingly, doubt whispering in her mind as she thought about her growing relationship with Chuck.

It had been two weeks since the fateful night she'd danced for him and then kissed him so passionately, and he still didn't know that she was also Fatima, the belly dancer. She had been out with him twice since, and both dates had been pleasant and enjoyable, although he hadn't touched her with the passion she knew him capable of. Meanwhile, as she felt more strongly about Chuck with every encounter, it bothered Faye that she'd been keeping the dancing a secret from him.

She longed to tell him the whole truth about herself but decided she couldn't do that—not after the way he had criticized Fatima. He'd thought her alter ego was a hooker, Faye recalled, so his opinion of her was bound to diminish if he found out about her dancing. But he had to find out sooner or later, she realized. But when? she wondered. And how? And what would it do to the fragile fabric of caring and affection that they were weaving between them?

Faye spent the next hour going over the Radbury account, jotting down a few things she thought could be done differently. The records were fine for the most part, but Chuck and his team had capitalized the intangible drilling costs when it would be to the company's advantage to deduct the costs outright. Faye didn't consider it a major problem, knowing it could be changed easily.

She glanced at her watch and was about to call it a day when Chuck burst through her door, an exasperated expression on his face. "Radbury wants to meet with us at nine in the morning," he said. "And he wants to discuss his tax situation with you then. I just thought I'd warn you that we'll have to work late tonight."

Faye thought of the dancing job she'd scheduled for eight and shook her head. "Not tonight, I'm sorry," she said. "I'm half through with his account already. If you can reschedule it for ten or eleven—"

"Faye, I can't do that," Chuck cut in. "He's leaving on a plane for Tulsa at ten thirty. Look, I'm sorry, but I'll feed you afterward."

"Chuck, I just can't stay late tonight," Faye protested, thinking of the birthday party at which Fatima would be the highlight. Chuck looked at her strangely, and Faye knew he was wondering why she was objecting so strenuously to a perfectly reasonable request. Come on, girl, think fast, she told herself.

"I promised an elderly friend that I would go by the nursing home and visit with her awhile," she began, amazed to hear herself lying so calmly. "I have to go. You know how elderly people can work themselves into a fuss when you don't show up. I'll take the work home and call you from there if I have any problems. All right?"

"Of course, and I think that's really nice of you. You want me to drive you over to the nursing home and wait for you while you talk to your friend?"

"Uh, no, the home's just a block from my house," Faye prevaricated. She looked at her watch and grimaced. If she was going to make the party on time, she had to leave quickly. "Is that all right?"

"Sure, I understand," Chuck said, smiling gently at her. "See you in the morning." He walked to the door and opened it, then turned back. "I guess you know you're something else," he said softly, then shut the door behind him.

Yes, Faye, you are certainly *something else,* she thought as a hearty twinge of guilt pricked her. You're a liar, you're a sneak, you're a— Oh, you can't wait to get out there and dance your little fanny off and you know it! she thought, grinning. She gave Chuck another minute to get to his office, then grabbed her purse and rushed out the door.

Chuck stuck his head into Faye's office a few minutes after she'd left. "Faye?"

"She's already gone, Mr. Goodall," Darlin said as she walked up the corridor with a handful of papers. "These need your signature."

Chuck nodded and stepped into Faye's office. "I'll use Faye's desk, since I don't want to have to walk all the way back to mine," he said as he sat down. He pushed aside her briefcase, then with a sinking feeling lifted the lid and spotted the Radbury account on top. "Uh-oh, she forgot her briefcase, and she's going to need these papers tonight."

Darlin's face creased into a frown. "That's not like her, is it?" she asked.

Chuck shook his head. "But she was looking forward to seeing a very dear friend tonight," he said. "Tell you what. I've got a couple more hours of work here, then I'll just run this by her place. Do you have her address?"

"I'll get it for you," Darlin volunteered, and hurried out of Faye's office.

Chuck looked at the briefcase and smiled. Faye was such a nice person, he thought. Imagine, going to see an elderly friend tonight, as busy as she was.

Finishing his work in record time, Chuck carried both his briefcase and Faye's to his car. He whistled under his breath as he drove toward Faye's condo. In fact, he wasn't particularly worried about the Radbury account or the briefcase—he was using this trip as an excuse to see Faye again, even though he'd been in and out of her office all day long.

He parked in front of her condo and rang her doorbell once, then twice. When Faye didn't answer Chuck got back into his car and rolled down the window. Since Faye had gone to see an elderly friend, he thought, she wouldn't be out that much longer. He would just wait for her.

Faye flashed her best smile as she tossed her hips up and down with the frenzied beat of the music. She laughed out loud as the boisterous group of college men shouted and clapped. This is great! she thought as she looked around at the happy crowd whistling and stomping its approval. Spurred on by their enthusiasm, she danced with that much more zest, her hips gyrating and her stomach popping in and out with the sense-jarring motion that seemed to fascinate the audience so much.

She was dancing to a different record tonight than when she had danced for Chuck—the music faster, less sensual, requiring less of her soul but a lot more of her body. The college men were not as interested in being seduced by her grace and beauty as being awed by her ability to move her body in fascinating ways. Understanding this, Faye gave them what they wanted, performing every difficult movement she knew, moving in ways that made people swear that she had different muscles and nerves than they did.

She clapped her finger cymbals and swirled her scarves until the lively twenty-minute recording was over. After bowing to the whistling, stomping, cheering audience, she exited but returned to take her usual bows. She refused the money one overeager young man tried to stuff in her skirt but did drink a quick beer with the appreciative men before leaving the fraternity house.

Faye started the car and the air conditioner, but folded her hands across the steering wheel and rested her head for a moment before putting the car in gear. She had almost been late tonight, and this was the first opportunity to relax since leaving the office over three hours before.

After fighting the horrible rush-hour traffic for the better part of an hour, she'd taken a quick shower, washed her hair, dried it, and set it in hot rollers to make it stand out from her head in wild disarray. She had pulled on her costume and done her elaborate makeup job as quickly as she could, remembering her mole at the last minute. Cursing the clock, she'd glittered and sprayed her hair and wasted a precious few minutes gluing a brand-new smoky quartz into her navel, which she now sorely regretted because the glue was sticking to her skin and pulling painfully. Then she'd driven the short distance to the fraternity house, appearing just in time.

I've got to get organized better, Faye told herself as she drove slowly toward her condo. She had loved dancing at the fraternity house. She always loved the dancing once she was performing, but sometimes just getting to a job was tiring, especially if she had to rush as she had tonight. She laughed at the confused stare she received from the driver in the car next to hers. When she had first started dancing, Faye had taken her outfits and dressed at the party, but now she felt it easier to dress at home and brave the startled reactions of her fellow drivers. Whatsamatter, buddy, don't you see a belly dancer driving a car every day? she said silently as she winked and waved at the surprised driver.

Looking forward to a hot shower and a cozy bed, Faye

turned the corner and stared in horror at the car parked in front of her condo. That's Chuck's Olds, she thought as she took in the big brown car in her driveway and the familiar head behind the wheel. She hit the brakes and put the car in reverse, backing around the corner and driving down to the next block, where she parked in front of the condo behind hers. What was Chuck doing there? Faye wondered, then groaned. The briefcase. Of course, he was returning the briefcase.

She sat for a while and considered her options. She could just drive up and brazen it out, but then Chuck would not only know that she was Fatima, he would know she'd lied to him. No, that was out, she decided. Stay all night with Ray and Carol? No, that was even worse: No telling how long Chuck would wait for her, and spending the night away from home would look even worse. Besides, she needed her briefcase. Could she cover the costume with a coat or something? she wondered. Oh, Faye, come off it, she thought. You're stuck as long as you're in this costume.

No, wait, that was it! She could go to the studio where she taught dancing and wash her face and change there! Jubilantly she started her engine, but then remembered she had nothing at the studio to change into. Faye muttered out loud and killed the engine. It would have been so easy!

But maybe it still would be, Faye thought as she eyed the small space between the two condos that were backed up to hers. Why not slip into her apartment from the back and sneak out with a pair of jeans and a shirt? she asked herself. Then, when she drove up half an hour later, it would seem she was returning from the nursing home. Right on, Faye, she thought as she got out of the car and scurried through the yard and between the two condos.

Gripping her house keys in her palm, she eased open the gate of her redwood fence and slipped into her small yard, then shut the gate behind her, being careful not to bang it. She made her way to her back door and slid her key into the lock, her heartbeat drowning out the noisy ping that signaled the opening of the locking mechanism. She stepped inside and again pulled the door shut, but did not close it completely behind her, then hurried across the kitchen and stepped smack in Lenore's water dish. Gasping with shock, Faye felt herself start to slide across the floor, now slippery with water. She grabbed for the counter and caught herself, but her hands were damp with sweat and unable to grip the slick edge of the counter, so the counter slid out of her grip and Faye landed on the floor with a thump. The water dish slid across the floor in the opposite direction and smacked against the wall with a loud crash. Faye froze at the sound. Could Chuck have heard the dish hit the wall? She sat still for a moment, then shook her head. No, she decided, he couldn't have heard the sound from the front seat of his car.

Groaning, Faye got to her feet, rubbed her sore bottom, then edged her way across the floor and out of the kitchen. Straining to see in the darkened rooms, she prayed there were no obstacles on the path to the bedroom. She crossed the living room, cursing herself for not shutting the curtains earlier, then slunk through the hall and into the bedroom.

The drapes were open. If Chuck happened to be looking in her direction, she thought, he'd see everything in the room. Cursing the dim moonlight filtering through the window, she got down on her knees and crawled across the room, her skirt catching on the carpet and her coins jangling around her breasts and hips. She crawled up to the dresser and eased open the top drawer, where she kept her knit shirts. She felt around, pawing through handfuls of lacy undergarments, but could not put her hands on a shirt. Oh, no, could they all be dirty and in the hamper? she wondered.

Beads of sweat breaking out on her forehead, she shut the drawer as quietly as she could and opened the one next to it, wincing when the moonlight illuminated her fingers. No shirts there either. She shut the drawer, flinching when it made a banging sound, and pulled open the one beneath it. A thorough inspection revealed nothing there either. Finally, close to the screaming point, Faye located a pair of jeans and a shirt in the bottom drawer. Breathing a sigh of relief, she crawled across the floor, not bothering to shut the drawer, and got to her feet in the hall. A quick trip into her bathroom yielded her sandals and a towel.

She breathed a sigh of relief while making her way back through the darkened house. She knew she couldn't risk staying in the condo any longer. *If I can just sneak out the back and over to the studio,* she thought, *I'll be home free!*

Chuck lit a cigarette and checked the luminous dial of his watch. It was already nine thirty, and there was no sign of Faye. Where on earth could she be this late? he wondered. Had she gone back downtown to get her briefcase? Maybe he shouldn't have been so quick to walk out with it, if it meant that she was at the office searching for it. But surely, even if she had gone back down there, he thought, she wouldn't be this late coming home.

Drawing deeply on the cigarette, Chuck loosened his tie and opened the door of his car. If it was already this hot in May, what was the summer going to be like? he wondered. The warm breeze was cooler than the stuffy confines of the car, so Chuck got out and walked to the front step, dusted off the welcome mat and sat down to enjoy his smoke. He considered leaving the briefcase on the front porch, but worried about something happening to the Radbury papers. No, he would just have to wait for Faye to come home, he decided, no matter how late she stayed out. He took one last drag from the cigarette and crushed it under his heel. She must have gone by the grocery store on her way home, he thought as he stared out at the warm, starry night.

Hearing a muffled crash from somewhere behind him, the hair on the back of his neck stood up. He whipped around and stared at Faye's front door. Had the sound come from inside Faye's house? he wondered. He listened, straining his ears, but no other sound emerged from the dark condo. No, it must have been his imagination, he thought. Still, it wouldn't hurt to take a look.

He got up and walked around the side until he reached the wall joining Faye's condo to the one next door, then retraced his steps until he had returned to the front step. He started to sit back down, but an instinct prompted him to walk around the house. He peered briefly through the living room windows, then continued on to the windows of Faye's bedroom, his eyes piercing the darkness for any sign of life. He was about to return to the porch when he spotted what looked like an open drawer at the bottom of the dresser. Thinking that it looked suspicious, Chuck retraced his steps and peered into the living room window again, where he glimpsed what looked like a figure rushing through the room and out of sight.

She's being robbed! he thought, and ran around the corner and smack into the wall between the condos. Swearing loudly, he backed off and rubbed his smarting forehead,

62

then continued to the back of the house and jerked open the gate, giving no thought to his own personal safety. That thief was *not* going to rob Faye! he told himself.

Meanwhile, Faye had rushed back through the darkened house and into the kitchen. Easing her way across the wet floor, she pushed open the back door and peered outside. Seeing no one, she stepped outside and locked the door behind her. She was crossing the yard when she heard a faint thump and the sound of someone approaching.

Who could it be? she wondered, freezing. It's Chuck! she thought. I have to get out of here before he sees me! As she continued across the yard, she saw out of the corner of her eye that her other gate—the one that led to the front yard —was open, and glimpsed the dark figure of a man come through it. Seeing her, he let out a blood-curdling yell and bolted toward her.

Faye's conditioning as a dancer suddenly came into play. She tore across the yard and into the narrow alley. Deciding she would have a better chance of eluding Chuck in the shadows, she darted down the darkened alley, deftly dodging trash cans and plastic bags full of garbage. She ran to the end of the block, across a small driveway, and into an alley on the next block. The hard asphalt stung her poorly protected feet and her billowing skirts and scarves impeded her progress. But she was fit, and confident she could elude Chuck. She *had* to elude him! she thought.

Chuck had stared at the strangely clad figure running across Faye's yard, cradling a bundle in his arms and tinkling faintly in the evening quiet. What on earth did the robber have on? he'd wondered. Was he a member of a cult? Shaking his head, he hesitated only a moment before letting out a yell that was supposed to freeze the robber in his tracks, but the strangely-garbed figure just seemed to be that much more determined to escape. I guess robbers don't freeze in their tracks, Chuck thought as he tore across the small yard in pursuit of the villain.

Looking both ways, he spotted the figure several houses down, running for dear life. Well, that's all right, buddy, Chuck thought as he sprinted after the robber. I bet I last longer than you do! He ran to the end of the block, across a small driveway, and into the next alley, where he stopped and stood quietly. He'd completely lost sight of the running figure. He stared into the gloom, straining his eyes for a flash, a motion, straining his ears for the faintest sound. Surely the robber hadn't run away that quickly! he thought.

Faye stood frozen against the wall between two condos and tried to control her erratic breathing. Chuck hadn't run past her as she'd hoped he would. Instead, he'd stopped and he was staring around the alley as though he could tell that she wasn't very far away. Go on, Chuck, she urged. Run after me. Go down the alley. But he merely waited, then turned in a slow circle and stared into the darkness, right at her. Faye gulped and held her breath. *Oh, please don't see me.* His eyes scanned a wide circle, then he shrugged and headed back into the driveway.

Attaway, Chuck, Faye thought as she released the pent-up breath she'd been holding. Go back to the house. Look down the next block. She leaned against the wall and took a steadying breath. I'll give him a few minutes just to make sure, she thought as she stared into the dark. I'll just make sure he doesn't come back. She gave him a good five minutes, then started to slowly back out from between the houses. Her car was parked on the next block. With a little luck, she thought, she would be there in a moment.

"Gotcha!" a deep masculine voice roared in her ear as

two strong hands gripped her upper arms. Faye let out with a blood-curdling yell and threw her clothes up in the air, then started to twist and pull at the assailant who held her in his grip.

Chuck held her arms tightly and marched her out from between the condos, then whirled her around and stared into her pale, frightened face. "My God, you're a woman!" he exclaimed. "A woman in a belly dancing costume! Well, if that doesn't beat all! Isn't that garb a little strange to be wearing to rob people in?"

"Let me go!" Faye demanded in a strangled voice.

"No, ma'am," Chuck said as he marched her down the sidewalk and across the driveway. "You were robbing my friend and you have to face the music."

"Don't be ridiculous!" Faye hissed. "Let me go, Chuck."

Chuck froze in his tracks, then increased their pace until they reached her front yard. He pulled her under a street-light and stared into her upturned face. "Faye? My God, is that you?"

"Yes, of course it's me," Faye replied. "Who else would want my jeans and shirt?"

"Do you have a way to get in, or did you throw away your keys too?" he demanded.

"No, I managed to hang on to the keys," she replied as she pulled away and rubbed her upper arms.

Finding the proper key, she unlocked the front door. Chuck pushed her in the front door and shut it behind her, then fumbled around in the dark until he found a light switch and flooded the room with light. He turned around and stared incredulously at the woman who stood before him, a defiant expression on her vivid face.

Chuck's face paled and he swallowed visibly. "Fatima!"

he said softly as he gazed at the woman before him, her dishevelment only adding to her sensual allure. He stared at her slowly, incredulously, taking in the sensuous, revealing costume, the wild array of hair that tumbled down her back and around her face, the bare waist and midriff. "My God, you're Fatima," he whispered as he shook his head as though to clear it.

"Yes, I'm Fatima," she replied quietly, a touch of pride in her voice. Despite the great lengths she had gone to conceal her identity, now that he knew she was Fatima, she found herself perversely proud of it.

"You're a belly dancer?" he demanded.

Faye's head shot up. "Yes, I am a belly dancer," she ground out. "And I'm a damn good one, as you well know."

"I can't believe it!" Chuck exclaimed as he raked her with scornful eyes. "A belly dancer, for crying out loud!"

"And what's wrong with being a belly dancer!" Faye demanded, furious at Chuck's contempt. She advanced on him with fire in her eyes. "What's wrong with being a dancer, pray tell? You enjoyed me enough the other night once you stopped your blushing!"

As she bore down on him, he moved back, stumbled down the step into her sunken living room, and fell backward, landing on the carpet with a soft whump. Then he jumped up, glowering at the grin on Faye's lips, and plopped down into one of her plush chairs. Faye followed and sat down across from him. Chuck glared at her across the narrow space.

"I guess you and Ray had a ball setting me up," he accused her. "Let's play a fast one on old-maid Chuck, the straight-arrow. Let's embarrass him good this time."

"Oh, sure," Faye scoffed. "Sure, I'm going to pull a fast

one on you by dancing for the man I have to work with. Don't you see, Chuck? Ray set us both up! Do you think I would have danced for you and kissed you like that if I had known who you really were? Ray had a good laugh at both of us."

Chuck looked across at the sensual, alluring face—Fatima's face. Why hadn't he noticed it before? he wondered. The features were Faye's behind the makeup. But it had been dark that night, and then, even in the bright light of Faye's living room, Fatima possessed a riveting sensuality only hinted at in the calm demeanor of Faye Catalini. The hair, the figure, the smoldering eyes—these belonged to Fatima, but now they belonged to Faye, too, the Faye he had found himself growing so fond of. He looked into her eyes and felt himself drowning in their depths.

"Are you telling me the truth?" Chuck demanded. "Are you sure you and Ray didn't plan it together beforehand?"

Faye shook her head, her dark hair bouncing around her face. Her eyes radiated honesty. "No, I've already told you, I wouldn't do that to you or myself. I didn't set you up, Chuck."

"So what were you doing tonight?"

"I was trying to sneak in and get some clothes. I was going to change at the studio and come back," Faye admitted guiltily.

Chuck leaned back in his chair and studied her critically. "Just a wee bit dishonest, aren't you?" he asked.

"I had to be," Faye replied, her lips set in a tight line.

"Why?" Chuck demanded. "If you didn't know who I was at the party, why didn't you tell me who you were when we met the next morning?"

"Are you kidding?" Faye asked. "First off, I thought all

67

morning that you and Ray had set *me* up . . . ! That you knew who I was and were just playing with me."

"And after you knew the truth?" Chuck asked quietly.

"Even more impossible. Look, you know that if my dancing were to become public knowledge, my accounting days would be over. Tax managers simply do *not* belly dance. How do you think old man Wilson would take that kind of news?"

"Hopefully sitting down," Chuck admitted. He looked at her contemptuously. "I simply can't believe you're Fatima." He slapped the chair with the palm of his hand. "I can't believe a woman like you would do a thing like that! Why didn't you tell me?"

"Why do you think? You sat there while Ray teased you, as embarrassed as an old maid at a dirty movie, and then you had the gall, the *unmitigated gall,* to accuse Fatima of being a hooker!"

"Well, is she?" Chuck sneered. "Does she kiss everybody the way she kissed me?"

Faye paled at the insulting taunt. "And what if she were?" she taunted back at him. "What if she does? Maybe a stuffy prude like you could use one to teach him a thing or two!"

Chuck sucked in his breath at the insult, then his eyes narrowed, and before Faye could move out of the way, he grabbed the bodice of her costume and jerked her up out of the chair, standing with her between the chairs. Angrily, he clamped his mouth down on hers, forcing her lips open. Faye struggled and tried to pull away, but Chuck was strong, his anger making him even stronger, so all she could do was squirm uncomfortably against his hard, taut body. He anchored her head with one hand while the other drifted down her shoulders to tease the soft flesh at the top of her bodice.

He withdrew his lips a fraction and whispered down at her. "So you think I need a hooker to teach me how to make love? Lady, you've got another think coming!"

This time Chuck did not insult Faye with a kiss of anger. He met her lips tenderly, passion just barely leashed under his sensual assault as he outlined her lips with the tip of his tongue. Slowly, as he worked his magic, Faye's anger faded and she opened her lips to his, letting him past the ivory barrier into the moist sweet depths, her own tongue snaking out to meet his.

She knew she had hurt him deeply with her accusations, and that this was his way of proving her wrong. Her own hands uncurled from their tight fists and crept up around his neck, where they found the soft hair at his nape and curled into the ends of it. Chuck let his hand slide down the satiny material of her bodice, where she could feel him caressing her breast through the layers of gauze that separated them. Sweet, sweet, Faye thought as she ran her hands down his muscled shoulders and around his back to his hard waist. She anchored him to her, loving the feel of his hard masculinity against her hips. This is madness, she thought, wondering what kind of spell had captured them.

Chuck's fingers trembled as they sought the tender sweetness of her breast, then his fingers found the end of the scarf that shielded her breast from his questing touch. He pulled out the scarf, then lightly palmed her tender bud, and it grew hard in his hand as Faye trembled beneath him. His anger wasn't gone but it was temporarily banked; he admitted to himself that he had wanted this to happen every day since Fatima had danced for him two weeks ago. He had wanted to kiss her, to touch her, to hold her in his arms.

But he wasn't just holding Fatima in his arms, he was holding Faye Catalini too. Proper, businesslike Faye. The Faye he was growing to like so much. With trembling fingers he thrust Faye away from him as his face hardened. Caught in the vortex of passion, Faye looked momentarily confused, the desire that had transformed her face into exquisite beauty evaporating, a look of anger and wariness surfacing.

"Well, how was that?" he taunted. "Still think I need a hooker to show me the ropes?"

Faye straightened the legs that threatened to buckle under her from the effect of passion and the pain of rejection. She took a deep breath and looked him in the eye. "It's a shame you're too prim to kiss Faye like that," she said coldly. "She might have liked it as much as Fatima does."

Chuck paled at her insult, then stormed out the door, slamming it behind him. He threw it back open a moment later and slammed her briefcase down in the entryway. "If you can get out of your harem getup, we still have to meet Radbury in the morning," he reminded her, then slammed the door a second time.

As Faye picked up the briefcase and laid it on the couch, she thought back on what had just happened. He took it worse than she had thought he would. But she hadn't been any better, she mused. She had insulted him about his primness—the shyness that he didn't seem able to help—and that had been cruel and uncalled for.

Or had it been? she asked herself as she sank down in the chair and put her head in her hands. He had acted as if her dancing were something shameful, and then asked her if she was a hooker. He had no right to say that, she wailed inwardly as the hurt she felt made itself known in the two tears that snaked down her face.

Faye picked up the briefcase, popped it open and removed the folder. Was there any point in even studying it? she wondered. Was Chuck going straight to Mr. Wilson in the morning with the news of her interesting part-time job? He wouldn't do that to me! she thought frantically as she stared at the figures in front of her. At least, she hoped he wouldn't.

Chuck sank back in the cushions of his sofa and stared at the empty fireplace across from him. He swallowed a sip of his much-needed Scotch and soda and kicked off his scuffed shoes. So much for playing the gallant and rescuing Faye's stolen property! he thought. It seemed he'd made a fool of himself, first by chasing her down, then by kissing her as he had. But he had only been trying to do the right thing when he chased her, he told himself as he remembered his alarm upon seeing the fleeing figure. He'd thought her a robber. And when he'd kissed her, he was angry with her for the deception she had carried out.

But as Chuck sipped his drink, he had to admit that he was more than angry. He was surprised and disappointed too. He'd really started to like Faye Catalini, and the knowledge that she was also Fatima, the sensuous belly dancer, had shaken him to his core.

Not that there was anything all that bad about the dancing, he thought. Sure, her dancing was highly sensual, but it was not dirty or sleazy or cheap. If it had been any other woman, Chuck would have said, "Right on." But it wasn't just any woman who danced like that, he mused—it was Faye, which bothered him more than he liked to admit. It

71

wasn't the dancing that bothered him as much as what the dancing revealed about Faye.

Chuck leaned back and let his memory replay the sensuous dance she had performed for him on his birthday. He shut his eyes and watched her dance in his mind. Fatima was abandoned and erotic in her movements, enticing him with every motion of her delightful body. A woman would have to be wild, sensual, and uninhibited to let herself dance like that, he thought. And that wild, uninhibited woman was really Faye.

Chuck opened his eyes and sipped morosely at his drink. Why couldn't Faye have been what she first seemed to be? he asked himself. Quiet and proper, businesslike, calm—a good match for a quiet, shy accountant like him. He had hoped that maybe, eventually, a relationship with her would be possible. But now it seemed to him it would never happen. She would find him dull, boring, a real drag. Just as his ex-wife, Julie, had.

Chuck finished his drink and let his mind wander over a few of the painful memories Julie had left behind. She was a schoolteacher, more striking than beautiful, and at first they had been reasonably happy. But Julie had teased him unmercifully about his staid clothes and his staid job and his staid lifestyle. She wanted to go to wild parties and dance until dawn and make love out in the backyard under the sprinkler. Chuck had tried to live up to her expectations, but he was never really comfortable with most of them, and although Julie never complained, Chuck suspected she found their sex life lacking too. Julie had tried as hard as he had, but her restless, uninhibited spirit had gotten worse, not better, as the years passed. Eventually she had gotten involved with a traveling photojournalist who entertained her for hours with stories of his exploits in the war-torn areas of the world. She was sorry, she had said, but for the first time in nearly ten years she felt truly alive, and she wanted her freedom.

Chuck sighed and finished the rest of his drink. He had tried hard to make Julie happy, but the plain truth was that she found him dull. He sat up and plopped his stockinged feet on the floor. And if Julie had been restless and unsatisfied with him, could he honestly hope to satisfy a wild, sensual, erotic woman like Fatima? he thought. No, he couldn't. He couldn't possibly make a woman like that happy.

Chuck swirled the ice cubes in the tumbler and contemplated fixing another drink, but decided against it. He was too upset to sleep well, and he didn't want to add a hangover to the tiredness he would be feeling in the morning. Besides, he was never one to drink himself into numbness. He sighed and stared up at the plastered ceiling. He was never one to do a lot of things. He would never storm a woman's defenses and take her masterfully into his arms, unless he was as angry with her as he'd been tonight. He was slow and predictable, at least that was what Julie had said, and he doubted seriously that he would ever be any different.

That isn't the kind of man Faye needs, he thought sadly. She needs one of those firecrackers, those macho men who can sweep her off her feet. Chuck stared up at the ceiling, knowing he could never be that man. Why are the cards always stacked against me? he asked himself angrily as he got up from the couch and made his way to bed.

Faye glanced at her watch, then knocked on the door to Chuck's office. It was almost time to go home, and she'd never been more grateful for a day to be over. She had been on pins and needles all day, waiting for Mr. Wilson to fire her for belly dancing as Fatima, but the day had passed and no word had been sent. Mercifully, she had received an early call from Darlin informing her that Jay Radbury had cancelled their meeting and rescheduled it for next week, so she had been spared having to face Chuck in the morning.

She was sure that tonight's date was off, that Chuck didn't want to spend any more time with a woman whose morals he questioned, and it disappointed her. They hadn't seen or spoken to each other all day, and she would have avoided this meeting entirely if she hadn't found a couple of things in the Radbury account that Chuck needed to correct before their rescheduled meeting.

At Chuck's muffled "Come in," Faye opened his door, stepped inside, and pushed it shut behind her. Chuck sat behind his desk, his tie straight, his three-piece suit buttoned, not a hair out of place. The perfect accountant, Faye thought as a wave of irritation rolled over her. Their argument the night before hadn't bothered him at all, it seemed. She sat down in one of the chairs in front of his desk and handed him the Radbury account.

"I caught a couple of things you might want to change in here," she said, schooling her voice to be bland.

Chuck took the folder from her and Faye noticed the circles under his eyes that his glasses almost concealed. So he didn't sleep so well, either, she thought. Good! He opened the folder and Faye reached across the desk and pointed to an entry in the column. "Here's the only major mistake I found. The intangible drilling costs." She slid her finger down to where the entries were listed.

"So what's wrong with what I did?" Chuck asked.

He's going to be belligerent, Faye thought. She took one

74

look at his cool face and decided to tackle him head on. "You capitalized the intangible drilling costs," she said. "They should have been expensed."

"Why?" he demanded. "We capitalize all that kind of thing."

"But you qualify for a bigger deduction if you expense them," Faye explained patiently.

"That's a crock," Chuck replied heatedly. "Exploration and developmental expenses have been capitalized for years."

"But the law just changed this year," Faye went on, holding on to her patience with sheer determination. "You can save a bundle, thousands of dollars, if you'll deduct them directly."

"You don't know what you're talking about!" Chuck roared. "They're capitalized!"

"Deduct them!" Faye snapped, her own patience gone.

"I'll be damned if I'm going to listen to a woman who shakes her butt at night for the world to see!" Chuck roared back. "What the hell do you know about it, anyway?"

Faye's face paled in fury, then she picked up the telephone and dialed Ray's extension. Her voice tight with anger, she spoke into the telephone. "Ray? This is Faye. You've done tax before, right? Will you settle a point for Chuck and me? He wants to capitalize the intangible drilling costs, I want to deduct them. What do you think? Deduct? Of course deduct. Thank you, Ray," she said sweetly.

She hung up the telephone, fire in her eyes as she focused on Chuck. "It just so happens, hotshot, that you were wrong, dead wrong. And I don't appreciate the crack about the dancing, either." She stood up and advanced on him, breathing fire, and jabbed her finger into his chest. "I dance but I do it on my own time, and it doesn't have a thing to do with my job here. *Nothing*, do you hear me?" Chuck, frozen in place by her deadly anger, nodded his head speechlessly. "And I never want to hear another crack about the dancing, ever again." He nodded and looked down at her finger, which she then removed.

Chuck watched her through narrowed eyes as her anger faded as quickly as it had grown. "You know, Chuck, I'm really disappointed in you," she said. "I thought, or I had hoped, you would be different, but you're not. You're just like every other accountant in the world."

"And how's that?" he asked.

"A male-chauvinist prig," she said sadly as she headed for the door. "And very unfair. Good night, Chuck."

Chuck watched her leave his office and shut the door behind her. He guessed that he ought to be angered by her accusation, but the dispirited way in which she had delivered it had stopped him. She had not said it in anger, but in sadness and regret. He ought to go after her, he thought, tell her that he was sorry, that the dancing didn't bother him. But he couldn't do that. His own insecurities kept him bolted to his chair, until he had given Faye plenty of time to leave the office.

Faye got into her car and pulled the door shut behind her. Tears of disappointment filled her eyes and ran down her cheeks as she started the engine and backed out of her parking slot. Why did Chuck have to be so narrow-minded about her dancing? she wondered. Why couldn't he have understood the other side of her nature? Faye sniffed and wiped the tears off her cheeks. Oh, stop crying and go on home, she told herself. You really didn't expect him to be any different, did you?

Once at home, Faye danced for two hours to the sensual beat of her music.

CHAPTER FOUR

"Here are the receipts Mr. Radbury sent over," Darlin said as she handed Faye a stack of papers. "His new assistant dropped them off. Boy, what a hunk!"

Faye took the papers from Darlin and stifled a laugh. "Nice-looking young man, hmm?" she asked as she glanced through the papers.

"Are you kidding? He makes Tom Selleck look like a wimp!" the girl enthused, her dangling gold earrings bobbing against her head. "Is that everything you need?" she asked as Faye put the papers in her briefcase.

"Yes, it looks like it," Faye said, and snapped the briefcase shut. "What time did Mr. Radbury schedule that meeting in the morning?"

"He wants to meet with you and Mr. Goodall at eight," Darlin said as she smoothed her beige linen skirt down her legs, the bangle bracelet on her wrist tinkling merrily. "Well, then, if you don't mind, I'm heading on out. I've got a date with a really super guy I met last week in that new disco."

"Have a good time," Faye said as Darlin headed toward the door, her thick blond curls bobbing behind her.

As Darlin reached the door, it flew open and Chuck came in, nearly colliding with her. He backed up hastily to give her clearance and smacked into the doorframe as Darlin's generous breasts brushed the front of his jacket. Faye bit her lip to smother a giggle as an embarrassed blush crept up his face, then felt a stab of jealousy that made her realize she wanted the opportunity to brush up against Chuck.

Chuck pulled away from the doorframe, shut the door behind him, then strode over to Faye's desk with a familiar ledger. "Here's the rest of the Radbury paperwork," he said stiffly as he handed her the ledger, careful not to touch her hand with his fingers.

Faye took the ledger and thumbed through it. "Everything here seems to be in order," she said. "I'll go over these tonight and call you if there's a problem."

"You're not going out?" Chuck asked.

Faye glanced up quickly, expecting to find sarcasm on his face but finding none. "No, I'm not dancing tonight," she said softly, lest anyone be walking by her door.

"I didn't mean—"

"But you wondered, and I told you," Faye said. "I'll do these tonight."

"Thanks," Chuck said abruptly. "I'll see you in the morning." He straightened his shoulders and left her office.

Faye leaned back in her desk chair and shut her eyes. I guess the cold war will be on forever, she thought as she rubbed the bridge of her nose. It had been two weeks since Chuck had discovered that her alter ego was Fatima, two *long* weeks. After the argument the next day in the office, Chuck had been very careful to defer to her superior knowledge of tax law. As a result their working relationship seemed fine, on the surface, but underneath, the strain was still there. They were cold and politely formal with one another, the delightful man Faye had been getting to

79

know disappearing behind a professional wall. But she realized she'd retreated, too, becoming the abrupt, professional Miss Catalini so alien to her true nature.

But the attraction was still there, Faye thought as she stuffed the ledger in her briefcase and headed out the door. At least it was on her part, and if the look she had caught a couple of times in Chuck's eye was anything to go by, he was still just as attracted to her as he had ever been. Oh, no, the chemistry had not evaporated just because he had found out about Fatima. Faye tossed her briefcase into the front seat and drove into the usual thick late-afternoon traffic, further snarled by a nasty thunderstorm. Chuck was trying to control it, they both were, and Faye realized that unless he changed his mind about her dancing, they would both just have to go on controlling it.

Faye changed out of her rain-dampened suit and danced in the living room for a few minutes while her TV dinner heated in the oven, then sat at the kitchen table with her dinner and a glass of iced tea while perusing Jay Radbury's receipts. When she'd finished her meal she took the ledger to her dining room table, where she often did her paperwork. She went over the ledger as she sipped iced tea and listened to the sound of the wind and the increasingly heavy rain, admiring the work Chuck and his department had done on their audit. I could shut this ledger right now and nobody would ever know the difference, she thought.

But Faye was too much of a professional not to check the books thoroughly, and she recalled the mistake Chuck had made two weeks before. So, settling in her comfortable chair, she spent a very dull two hours going through the books that Chuck and his department had prepared.

She'd gone through four glasses of iced tea and had come to the next to last page when her eyes widened. *What in the world?* She stared at the neatly printed figures and shook her head slowly. I don't believe this, she thought as she took out her calculator and rapidly punched in some numbers. She had found yet another batch of figures that should have been deducted directly.

The change would save Radbury a lot of money, she thought, carrying the ledger to the kitchen. She fished Chuck's card out of her wallet and punched out his number. She wanted to explain the mistake to him before changing the figures in the ledger.

Faye let Chuck's phone ring ten times, then hung up and tried again. He'd said he would be home and that she was to call him if she needed anything. She let it ring fifteen times, then hung up and dialed the operator. "Would you dial this number for me?" she asked. "My associate said he would be home tonight." Faye read off the number.

"Ma'am, I'm sorry, but all the phones in that exchange were knocked out by the storm," the operator said. "It sounds like they're ringing but they're not."

"Oh, no," Faye murmured. "How soon will they be restored?"

"It's hard to say, ma'am," the operator replied. "A major substation went down. It might not be fixed until the morning."

"Thank you," Faye said, hung up, and cursed. The meeting with Radbury was for eight in the morning, and she wouldn't have time to talk to Chuck before then.

She sat down at the dining room table and carefully painted over Chuck's errors with liquid paper. After the paper was dry she entered the new figures, matching Chuck's handwriting as closely as she could so that Jay Radbury would not realize a mistake had been made, and so that Chuck would not be embarrassed in front of him.

81

She then made her way through the rest of the records, more carefully than before. She tried to call Chuck when she'd finished the books, and again before she went to bed, but all she got on the line was a buzzing noise.

The next morning Faye opened her eyes to discover the sun was shining much more brightly than usual for six o'clock. She cursed even louder when she saw the numbers on her digital alarm clock flashing, discovering on her wristwatch that it was already after seven. Apparently her electricity had gone off sometime in the night, she thought, and Jay Radbury was a man that you *did not* keep waiting!

Faye raced out of bed, showered, dressed, and made up her face in twenty minutes flat, but she was still fifteen minutes late when she hurried into the conference room where Jay Radbury and Chuck were waiting.

"Sorry I'm late," she said as she opened her briefcase and withdrew the ledger. "My electricity was off for a while last night and my alarm didn't go off."

Jay Radbury nodded and blew a puff of acrid cigar smoke toward the door. "That's all right, Miss Catalini," he said as he took the ledger from her and flipped through it. "Nasty storm last night."

"Yes, my telephones were still out when I left this morning," Chuck said.

"I know. I tried to call you three times last night," Faye said, nudging Chuck's foot under the table. Chuck jumped and his eyes narrowed as he stared into Faye's face, composed in a bland expression. Who was she trying to play footsie with, him or Radbury? he wondered.

"Three times?" Chuck asked as he fought not to blush. What a time for her to pick to get fresh with him! he thought, edging his leg slowly away from hers.

"That's right," Faye said as she gave Chuck's leg a swift

82

kick with the pointed toe of one of her pumps. "I needed to ask you a question about the ledger."

So it wasn't footsie she was playing, Chuck thought as he rubbed the back of one leg against the shin she'd kicked. Faye must have been trying to warn him about something in the ledger, he realized, then caught her eye and nodded.

Jay Radbury made his way through the ledger page by page, finally coming to the next to last page. He squinted at the figures and scratched the top of his head. "I swear I don't remember these figures being this low," he said as he placed the ledger in front of Chuck.

They weren't, Chuck thought to himself as he looked at the altered figures. Good grief, there was nearly a two-hundred-thousand-dollar difference in Radbury's favor! "Uh, I'll let Faye explain this to you." And while she's at it she can explain it to me, too, he thought.

Faye took the ledger and ran her finger down the column of figures. "These construction-period taxes and interest are usually capitalized," she explained softly. "For financial purposes, the interim financing is amortized over the life of the loan, but it's actually more valuable to deduct the expense directly." She looked at Chuck. "We changed this a couple of days ago. It saved your company nearly two hundred thousand."

"Well, I'll be," Jay drawled as he stubbed out his cigar in the ash tray. Faye glanced over at Chuck and saw him quickly disguise an angry scowl. "I'll tell you, this firm has sure saved me a heck of a lot of money since I hired y'all." He closed the ledger and shook Faye's and Chuck's hands. "Thank y'all again," he said as he made his way to the door.

Faye leaped up and followed him to the door. "We'll

look forward to doing business with you again," she said as she followed him out the door and shut it behind her.

Chuck had appeared angry with her for making the changes, and she was in no mood to tangle with him this morning, so Faye disappeared into her office and shut the door behind her. She was soon immersed in the sticky tax problems of the takeover of a praline factory by an international conglomerate.

Chuck picked up the ledger and stared at the altered figures. How could he have made a stupid mistake like that? He could have cost Radbury nearly two hundred thousand dollars! And he would have, he thought, if it hadn't been for Faye's catching his mistake and correcting the error.

She knew her tax laws, he mused, and she was one gracious lady, too, he admitted to himself as he wandered back toward his office. She could have made it obvious that she'd caught him in a serious blunder. She could have taken all the credit for the change and made him look like a complete fool, but instead she not only warned him that something was not as it should be, she had been careful to word her response so it seemed they'd both made the change. And that was after he had practically accused her of being an immoral woman because she was also a belly dancer, and an incompetent accountant too.

Chuck sat down at his desk and stared vacantly at a stack of papers from a local real estate firm. He had been wrong to treat Faye the way he had, he thought. It was none of his business if she belly danced on her own time, and she deserved more from him as a colleague than chilly politeness.

Deciding he owed her an apology for the way he'd treated her the past two weeks, and also owed her a thank-you for bailing him out that morning, he got up to go to her office. But he stopped and sat back down. No, he would go by her place tonight, he thought, when they both had more time to discuss things privately.

Faye had pulled on her leotard and was just tying her hair back in a loose ponytail when she heard the doorbell ring. "Oh, no, I hope it isn't Myrtle Golden wanting to tell me about her arthritis again," she muttered as she pushed her feet into her dancing slippers. Most of the time she didn't mind listening to Myrtle's woes, but she had just barely ten minutes to spare if she was going to make it to dance class on time.

Faye tiptoed out into the entry and approached the fisheye in the front door. If the caller was Myrtle, she decided, she just wouldn't answer the door. Stifling her guilt, Faye peered through the viewer and jumped back when she saw a huge hazel eye surrounded by a tortoiseshell frame staring back at her, its shape distorted by the lens.

"Chuck, what are you doing?" she asked as she yanked open the door.

"Just wanted to make sure you could tell it was me," he teased as she stepped aside to let him enter. Puzzled by his unexpected appearance, Faye shut the door and motioned for him to sit down in the living room. He looked up and down at her in her leotard and ponytail and shook his head. "It looks like you were on the way out," he said. "I'll talk to you in the morning."

"I have ten minutes or so," Faye said as she sat down on the edge of the sofa. "Will that be enough time?"

"I don't know. How long does it take to say that I've been a real jerk and I'm sorry and thank you?" Chuck asked in a rush.

"Three-point-eight seconds," Faye said dryly as Chuck blushed. "So sit down and tell me about it. I thought you were furious with me this morning for changing the ledger."

"No, I was furious with myself for making that kind of stupid error," Chuck said as he sat down in the chair across from her. "Look, I appreciate you covering for me this morning and I thank you for that." He stopped and took a deep breath.

"And I'm sorry, I really am, for acting like I did when I found out that you were Fatima. I had no business acting that way. It sure doesn't have anything to do with your accounting. And I didn't mean what I said about the other . . ." he mumbled. "I don't think you're—well—you know."

"Thank you, Chuck," Faye said quietly. "That means a lot."

Chuck nodded. "Well, since you're on your way, I'll see you tomorrow," he said, trying hard to keep the disappointment he felt from showing on his face. He had hoped, by timing his visit early enough in the evening, that he might be able to prevail on Faye to go out with him for a pizza. "Are you dancing tonight?"

"No, I teach a class once a week," Faye said as she noted the crestfallen expression Chuck couldn't quite hide. "Say, are you busy tonight?"

Chuck shook his head.

"All right, then, how would you like to come along with me and watch the class?" she asked. "Or would it bother you to see me dancing?"

Chuck brightened. "I think I can make the sacrifice."

"Give me a minute to gather up something to change

86

into and I'll be right with you," Faye said, and she hurried to her bedroom.

She stuffed clean underwear and an uncrushable sundress into her dancing bag, then rejoined Chuck. Soon after, they were in his car, Faye directing him toward the health club where she taught a weekly class in the art of belly dancing.

Faye made her way through the noisy club and into one of the smaller rooms that led off the weight room. She motioned for Chuck to have a seat in the corner of the carpeted room and greeted the small group of women waiting for her. She led the group through a few warm-up exercises and then put on a record, the class performing a slow, sensual number.

She does it so beautifully, Chuck thought as he compared her flowing, graceful movements with the jerkier, more awkward movements of some of her pupils. The mirrors lining two of the walls made her every move, every wiggle, visible from both the back and the front at the same time. Chuck found himself watching Faye more and the other women less, her dancing weaving a magic spell around him. Even with her hair up in a ponytail and her face nearly devoid of makeup, he thought, Faye was Fatima. She didn't need the costume and the clappers in her hands. All she had to do was move to the music.

It had never occurred to Chuck the night she had danced for him that belly dancing wasn't easy, although she made it seem so. Now, as he watched the other women in the class trying to execute a difficult stomach roll that Faye could do effortlessly, he realized it must have taken her years to learn to belly dance as she did, and that she still must have to practice quite a bit to keep herself limber. As Chuck watched Faye lead the class through yet another dance, he had to admit she was a marvelous dancer and that her body in motion was a thing of beauty. If only the dance wasn't so sensual, he thought. As beautiful as it was, he still didn't feel comfortable with it.

Faye led the class through a few warm-down exercises, then they all sat on the floor while she showed them how she had made her latest costume from an old bikini bathing suit. She encouraged them to make a costume and try it out on their husbands or boyfriends, and promised that their zills—the tiny finger cymbals—would arrive in the mail by the next class.

As the women trooped out, Faye picked up her gym bag and wiped a hand across her sweating face. "Let me shower and change and I'll be right with you," she told Chuck.

"While you're in there, I want you to start thinking about what kind of pizza you want," Chuck said. "If you think you can work up an appetite for one, I'll take you."

"Are you kidding? After a class like this I could eat three pizzas," Faye admitted, and hurried toward the showers.

Faye quickly showered and dressed, and in a few minutes she and Chuck were seated across from one another in a booth at the local pizza parlor. They haggled for a few minutes over whether a pepperoni or a sausage pizza would ease their hunger pangs more efficiently, and on the advice of their waitress ordered a pizza that was half and half. Their waitress also brought them frosty mugs of beer.

Faye lifted hers and drank quickly. "Aah, that hits the spot," she said. "I'm always so thirsty after dancing."

"I can understand that," Chuck replied. "I'm always thirsty after running. And I'm sure the dancing's just as strenuous."

"It is, but in a different way," Faye said. "Running is very steady exertion. In dancing I speed up and slow down. You saw the way we were doing it this evening."

"I saw the way you were dancing and they were trying," Chuck quipped. "Some of them were all right but some of the rest—" He broke off his sentence and made a face.

Faye tried to frown at him but her face split into a grin. "Well, some women can do it and some can't." She laughed. "Last year I had this poor girl who tried and tried, and she still moved like a baby elephant when the class was over. But others do really well. Several of my former students are now dancing professionally." She stopped and sipped her beer.

"And the others?" Chuck asked.

"Oh, most of them have no intention of dancing professionally when they sign up. They just want to get a little exercise, or get their figures back in shape, or maybe add a little zest to a stale marriage."

Chuck raised his eyebrows. "I'm sure it could do that," he said dryly.

Faye shrugged. "So far I've had no complaints."

Chuck raised his mug to his lips for another swallow of beer. "What kind of women attend your class? I mean, they looked pretty much like a cross-section."

"They are," Faye replied. "About a third of them are full-time housewives. A few are students. The rest, surprisingly enough, are professional women. That class tonight included three teachers, two nurses, a real estate agent, a savings and loan vice-president, and a small-claims-court judge."

"But none of them will ever dance professionally," Chuck said. Faye shook her head as the waitress brought their pizza and set it in front of them.

89

Faye picked up a slice from the pepperoni half and took a bite. "Umm, this is delicious," she murmured.

Chuck took a bite of a sausage slice. "So is this, but don't eat all the pepperoni. I want to try a slice of it." He ate another bite, then took a sip of beer. "So how did you get started dancing?" he asked.

"For fun or for profit?" Faye asked as she bit off another chunk of the gooey pizza.

"Start at the beginning," Chuck suggested as he reached out and broke the strings of cheese that were trailing from his piece to the rest of the pie.

"Mama started me out in ballet classes when I was eight. I took ballet for a while and tap and modern dance also, and I was good, but I wasn't really interested in dancing as a full-time career. So in college I got my accounting degree, but I took dance classes at the same time, and in the middle of my sophomore year, a fraternity called my dance instructor with a request for a belly dancer. Well, three other girls and I found a belly dancer in New York City who was willing to give us a few lessons and we spent a weekend with her learning the basics." Faye stopped talking to take another bite of pizza.

"I presume you got through the first dance," Chuck said as he finished off his slice.

Faye nodded and laughed. "Just barely," she admitted. "We had about a five-minute routine, but that seemed to satisfy the boys. Anyway, after that I was hooked. I spent several more weekends with the instructor in New York and perfected the technique, dubbed myself Fatima, and made my availability known by word of mouth. I made almost enough in my senior year to pay my tuition. And it paid for my Master's degree."

"And after you graduated?" Chuck asked. "Didn't it interfere with your accounting career?"

"I've always kept it a secret," Faye admitted quietly. "From the first. Everywhere I've lived has been a big enough city that I could keep my identity as Fatima separate from my accounting career. At least I always have until now."

"Your secret's safe with me," Chuck told her. "But I don't understand. At first you needed the money, but that isn't the case any longer. So why do you do it? Why do you keep juggling the dancing and your other job? Why not quit dancing and just be an accountant?"

"But I didn't dance just for the money, even when I needed it," Faye explained as she swallowed the last of the beer in her mug. Chuck signaled the waitress to bring Faye a fresh mug. "I fell in love with the dance the first time I performed it, and I love it just as much today as I did ten years ago."

"But why belly dancing?" Chuck asked. "Why not ballet, or tap, or something like that?"

It was Faye's turn to blush. "Don't you know?" she asked. "Can't you tell? There's a side of me, a wild side, an emotional side. I guess it's my sensual side that needs an outlet, especially after spending my days as an accountant. And I have that outlet in belly dancing. Before I started belly dancing I was restless. But when I'm dancing I have a way to express my desire to be uninhibited and free."

Chuck swallowed and blushed. "I would never have guessed that first day in the office," he admitted. "You seemed so prim, so in control!"

"I am," Faye said. "And that's a legitimate side of my nature. But so is the other side," she added defiantly. "I have just as much right to be sensual as I do to be business-like."

"I didn't mean to say that you didn't," Chuck said quickly. "It's just that it's so unusual to find both qualities in one person." He picked up a piece of pepperoni pizza and bit off a chunk. "If you love the dancing so much, couldn't you give up the accounting and dance full time? Wouldn't you be happier?"

Faye shook her head. "Absolutely not," she said firmly. "If I did that, I wouldn't have an outlet for the intelligent, ordered, mathematical side of me. I *like* accounting! I need both, Chuck."

"So you intend to continue with both your accounting and your dancing," Chuck murmured, and sipped the fresh beer the waitress had brought him. "I just can't see how you can have two such radically different sides to your personality."

"That's all right, most people would have trouble reconciling Faye and Fatima," Faye said slowly. She took a sip from her beer mug and looked at him forlornly. "You're no different. I don't really expect you to be able to, either." She picked up a slice of the sausage pizza and chewed it.

Chuck looked at her wistful face and bristled with righteous indignation. "Now you listen here, Miss Fatima Catalini! I am going to take exception to that last statement. You're wrong, dead wrong, if you think that I, Chuck Goodall, cannot accept the two vastly different but equally intriguing sides to your nature. I only hope that Fatima is ready to take me on!" He opened his mouth to continue, but Faye burst out laughing and he joined her.

"No, seriously, Faye," Chuck said when their laughter abated. "I know that I reacted badly at first, and for that I'm just as sorry as I can be. But I've had a while to think about it and I think I can get used to the dancing, and this other side of you. I've missed you a lot these last two weeks."

"I've missed you too," Faye admitted.

"Anyway, I'd like to try," Chuck said. "Are you free on Saturday night?"

Faye thought a moment. "Yes, I'm free. I'm not dancing that night."

"Wonderful. We'll set a time and a place later. Now, if we intend to stay awake at the office tomorrow, I'd better get you home. It's after ten."

Faye nodded. Chuck paid the check and a few minutes later they were pulling up in front of her condo. Faye turned around and began to slide across the seat toward Chuck, but he jumped out of the car and started around to her side. Well, so much for a good-night kiss! Faye thought. We're back to Faye and Chuck and pecks on the cheek.

Chuck opened the door on the passenger side and reached for her hand. Gently he pulled her out of the car and tucked her arm into his, then he led her up to the front porch and waited patiently while she fumbled for her key. Finally she unearthed it in her gym bag, unlocked the door, and pushed it open.

"Well, good night," she said as she stepped inside.

To her surprise, Chuck stepped in behind her and shut the door. Faye looked at him with surprise. "Don't want to put on a show for the neighbors," he said. "Did you mean it when you said that Faye liked getting kissed as much as Fatima?" he asked.

Faye nodded, her eyes wide.

"Then I guess Faye won't mind if I kiss her good night," he said as he lowered his lips to hers, touching them gently once, twice, then his lips locking onto hers and capturing their sweetness in a stunning bond.

Too surprised for a moment to even respond, Faye finally raised her arms and slid them around Chuck, snaking her fingers through the thick brown hair at the nape of his neck. Her body pressed itself closer to his, and she savored the tautness of his arms and the warm hardness of his chest. Chuck groaned as he slid his arms around her, then with one swift motion he picked her up and carried her to the couch, without breaking off the kiss. He settled her down beside him and slid his hands around her waist as her arms slid down his shoulders to the hard warmth of his chest.

Chuck finally lifted his lips from hers and trailed a path of soft, moist kisses across her cheek and over one ear. "You feel so good in my arms," he murmured quietly as Faye explored his neck with feathery kisses. With gentle fingers she reached up and took his glasses off and dropped them on the cushions, then pressed soft kisses onto his eyelids.

"You feel good to me too," Faye said as she trailed her hands down the front of Chuck's shirt. And he did, she thought. He felt hard and warm and strong and exciting, and she wanted to touch him without the fabric barrier that separated them.

Boldly, daringly, she unbuttoned the top button of his shirt and planted a small kiss on the pale, hair-flecked chest that was exposed. Chuck flinched when she slid open the second button, then relaxed and let her open the buttons of his shirt almost to his waist, kissing and caressing her way down his broad expanse of chest.

"Relax," she breathed when she felt Chuck stiffen at a

particularly daring caress. "Just let me touch you." She kissed and touched his chest and waist as he rained small kisses on her face and her neck.

Chuck looked down at Faye's straining breasts, the nipples hard under her revealing sundress. "I want to touch you, too, Faye," he said as her covered breasts brushed against his bared chest.

Faye stared up at his face, mingled with desire and shyness. "So touch me," she whispered as she reached out and took his hand. She placed it over her taut nipple and thrust herself against the warmth of his palm.

Chuck's shyness melted as he felt her breasts swell in his hand, and with almost reverent fingers he pushed the sundress off Faye's shoulders and down her body, baring her almost to the waist. He reached out, caressed the tip of one of her nipples with his finger and felt it harden. Slowly, he bent his head and touched her other breast with tender lips, and felt it, too, swell with desire. Faye shuddered as waves of longing shafted through her. Shy and quiet as he was, the mere touch of Chuck's lips on her flesh made her body sing.

They caressed and touched one another for long moments, then Chuck raised his head and planted a final kiss on her lips. "We don't want to go too fast too soon," he said as he pushed her away from his heated body and took a deep breath.

"You're right," Faye admitted reluctantly, pulling away and pushing her dress back up on her shoulders. "I'm not —we're not—"

"I know that," Chuck agreed as he buttoned his shirt. "We need to get to know each other a little better before we get too physical."

"I'm glad you feel that way," Faye said, and kissed him lightly on the lips.

Chuck felt around the couch for a minute. "Uh, can you see where my glasses went? I can't find them."

Faye delved between the cushions and unearthed the glasses. She peered through them, made a face, and handed them to Chuck. "Ugh, those definitely aren't just for your image, are they?"

Chuck shook his head as he put the glasses back on. "No, they do serve a purpose. Fatima would just be a blur without them." Chuck touched her lower lip with his fingertip, then got up.

Faye walked him to the door. "See you in the morning," she said as Chuck murmured good night.

Faye sat down on the couch and pressed her fingers to her tingling mouth. Her entire body was still trembling from the sensual mastery of Chuck's caresses. And to think he had been too shy to kiss her like that before! she thought. Thank goodness he was over that!

Her face creased into a frown as she stared across the living room at the contemporary painting of a nude on the opposite wall. Was Chuck going to be able to make good on his promise? she wondered. It was one thing to say he was going to be able to accept the dancing, and what it revealed about her, but it was another thing to be able to live up to that promise. What if he was just like the rest? she asked herself. What if he couldn't reconcile the intelligent, businesslike Faye that he knew at work with the wild, uninhibited, sensual Fatima who danced for all the world to see?

Faye kicked off her shoes and tucked her feet beneath her. Oh, I hope Chuck can make good on that promise, she thought. She hoped he could get used to her other side, the sensual, uninhibited side, the side he hadn't yet seen much of. Even though he was quiet, she mused, even though he was proper and shy, his kisses and caresses set her on fire.

CHAPTER FIVE

Faye leaned over the shoulder of one of the young accountants in the pit and stared at the computer console. "Miss Catalini, did I figure this correctly?" he asked.

Faye entered a couple of figures into the nearby console. Immediately the screen flashed the same set of numbers. "Yes, this looks great," she said as the younger accountant breathed a sigh of relief. "Figure these next two accounts the same way."

She left the young man busily entering figures and wandered out of the pit and into the hall, where she ran right into Darlin. Faye opened her mouth to say hello but her jaw dropped in astonishment before she could utter the words. "Wha-what have you done to your hair?" she stammered. Darlin's previously blond hair was now a vivid shade of red.

"Henna," Darlin said proudly as she ran her hand down the flaming tresses. "Isn't it gorgeous?"

"Um, yes, it is," Faye said as she continued to stare at Darlin. "Did you do it yourself?"

Darlin's hair shimmered as she shook her head. "No way! I went to the salon and had it done right. You know," she went on as she cocked her head to one side, "you ought to try some color on yours sometime. You'd look great as a redhead too!"

Ray and Chuck walked through the front door and Darlin turned around to them. "Say, Chuck! Don't you think Faye would look great as a redhead?"

Chuck's mouth flew open and he started to shake his head, but Ray nodded slowly. "She might at that," he said. Chuck opened his mouth to protest but Ray caught his eye and winked. "A deep rich auburn," he went on.

"And you ought to wear it down sometimes," Darlin went on. "You always have it pinned up!"

"I wear it down sometimes," Faye said. "Just not here."

"Yes, she's been known to let it down on occasion," Chuck said dryly. Ray snickered and Faye's face flamed.

"Well, if you want the name of my stylist I have his card in my wallet," Darlin said. "See y'all." She headed into the pit with the folders she was carrying.

Chuck and Faye turned toward their offices, but Ray shook his head and pointed into the pit. "Let's watch," he whispered as he gestured toward the open door.

Faye and Chuck watched through the open door as Darlin approached Warden Smith with the folders. He looked up and his bland smile of welcome turned into a look of wide-eyed astonishment. He mumbled something to Darlin and was rewarded with her tinkling laugh. A couple of the accountants in the pit looked up, stared, and leaned over to the next desk. Soon, every eye in the pit was on Darlin, who was blithely unaware of the stir her appearance had caused. One accountant spilled coffee on his papers, and Faye spotted another who hit the wrong button and wiped out a whole console of figures.

As Darlin turned toward the door, Ray grabbed Chuck and Faye by the arms and pulled them back. "Let's get out of here before she sees us watching," he whispered. The three of them ducked into Faye's office and dissolved into helpless laughter.

"Did you see the look on Warden's face?" Chuck whooped. "He couldn't believe it."

"You looked just as bad when you saw her," Faye teased. "It was all I could do not to laugh at you."

"That's all right, you were standing there with your mouth hanging open, and you had had time to recover," Chuck shot back.

Ray laughed. "I think Faye ought to get that card. Fatima would be great as a redhead."

"Hush! Somebody might hear you," Faye hissed.

"I don't know what you're worried about," Chuck said as he sat down in one of her chairs. "If Cox and Wilson can take Darlin, Cox and Wilson can take anybody."

Faye shook her head. "You know, I've wondered about that," she said. "I know I might take the propriety here at the office to an extreme, but Darlin apparently has no idea the stir her appearance here causes. And as far as I know, no one has ever said a word to her about it. Why hasn't Mr. Wilson said something? You know, suggest she leave those dangly gold earrings at home?"

Chuck shrugged his shoulders. "She's very good at her job, I guess."

Faye started to nod in agreement, but she looked over at Ray and spotted a wide grin on his face. "Ray, do you know something we don't know?" she asked.

Ray shook his head, but his eyes danced with amusement. "Now, what would I know that you don't?"

"Plenty," Faye said. "Come on, Ray. Give."

Ray leaned toward Faye and motioned Chuck closer. "She's the daughter of Wilson's mistress."

"*What?*" Chuck burst out.

100

"I don't believe it," Faye said. "Not Mr. Wilson!"

"You better believe it," Ray snickered.

"Anybody else, sure," Faye said. "But Mr. Wilson? Nice, grandfatherly Mr. Wilson?"

"That's the story I got from Stuart Cox," Ray said. "Wilson's sweetie apparently pressured him into hiring her daughter. And Mr. Wilson's terrified of saying something that will offend the girl or her mama."

Chuck started to chuckle. "Who would ever have believed it?" he laughed. "Old man Wilson with a mistress!" He laughed harder. "He sure doesn't look the type."

"Well, you can't always tell about people by looking," Ray said as he winked at Faye. "Look, keep that under your hats, will you? Wilson would skewer me alive if it ever got out." He picked up his briefcase and left the room.

"Like you said, you can't ever tell by looking," Faye said to Chuck as she sat down in her desk chair.

"I hope you won't do it," Chuck murmured.

"Do what?" Faye asked absently.

"Dye your hair red." Chuck walked over to her, reached out, and stroked the smoky black tresses that were carefully pinned up in a bun. "It's so pretty as it is."

"Oh, heavens, Chuck, I wouldn't touch it," Faye assured him, shuddering a little. "This hair's my pride and joy!"

"Glad to hear that," Chuck said. He touched the curling hairs at her nape, jerking his hand back when Faye's door flew open and Darlin strode in.

"Miss Catalini, have you seen— Mr. Goodall, there's a call for you on line three. Sorry." She backed out and closed the door behind her.

"I wonder what she thought she interrupted," Faye

asked dryly as Chuck punched in the line and picked up the phone.

"Charles Goodall here. Mother? How are you?" He paused and Faye could hear a voice speaking on the other end of the line. She started to get up but Chuck motioned her to sit back down. "And Dad? That's good. How's Grandma?" He perched on the side of Faye's desk. "She's better? I'm glad to hear that." Chuck paused and listened. "This weekend?" He glanced over at Faye. "Well, actually I did." He paused. "Of course, if this is the last chance you have to come for the next three months, I'd love for you to come." He looked at Faye again, ruefully this time. "No, I'm sure she'll understand. When will you get here?" Chuck wrote a time on Faye's scratch pad. "No, mother, you're not inconveniencing me at all. No, please come. I'll see you Friday afternoon. Good-bye."

Chuck put the receiver back in the cradle and looked at Faye. "My folks are coming this weekend," he said. "As much as I hate to, I'm going to have to cancel our date."

Faye's face fell before she could stop it, then she forced herself to smile. "That's all right," she said. "I understand. Isn't this a little late notice, though?"

"I guess it sounded that way, but Mom and Dad are going up to Boston to visit mother's sister for most of the summer, and this weekend's the last chance they'll have to bring Grandma to see me before they leave. Grandma's not well and I sure don't want to miss seeing her."

"Of course not," Faye murmured. "You're lucky to have your parents and grandmother. Is your grandmother going to Boston with your parents?"

Chuck shook his head and made a face. "No, they're not taking Grandma Goodall." He laughed at a private joke. "Not quite."

"Well, have a nice weekend," Faye said, trying and failing to mask her disappointment. She'd been looking forward to their date ever since the night they had shared a pizza and he'd kissed her so thoroughly. Well, that was all right, she thought. He'd ask her again. Hopefully she wouldn't be dancing.

Chuck sensed the disappointment she was trying to hide. "Say, we always go out on Saturday night anyway," he said. "Why don't you join us?"

"Oh, no, I don't want to horn in on a family get-together," Faye protested.

"Nonsense. We'll pick you up about seven. All right?"

Faye's face split into a wide smile. "All right," she said. "See you at seven."

What on earth have I gone and set myself up for? Chuck thought as he drove toward his modern bungalow in one of Houston's newer subdivisions. Who was going to turn up her nose the highest? he wondered. Free spirited Faye, or the impossibly stuffy Gladys Goodall? Chuck groaned as he turned the air conditioner in his car up another notch. And his father was no better. Benson Goodall was the epitome of a conservative, old-fashioned, small-town banker. What was he doing introducing them to Faye?

Chuck sighed and turned into the subdivision where he and Julie had bought their home three years before. It wasn't that his parents weren't good, or kind, or loving, he thought; they were. But they were also prim, proper, and stuffy in the extreme. Even *he* thought so, and if he thought that about them, what on earth would Faye think?

And what were they going to think of her? Well, she would hardly wear one of her dancing costumes to dinner, he mused, and with her passion for keeping her dancing a

103

secret, he doubted she would tell them anything about it. In fact, she would probably be every inch the proper accountant she was in the office, and his parents would like that Faye. Chuck nodded to himself: On second thought, maybe dinner would go all right. And besides, Faye and Grandma Goodall were bound to hit it off.

Chuck adjusted his tie and walked out of the bedroom, shutting the door behind him. Tonight's going to be fine, he assured himself as he entered the living room, where his mother and grandmother were waiting.

"Charles, you look wonderful," Gladys said as she reached out to straighten his tie.

Chuck smiled at his mother, admiring the elegant, patrician lines of her face. She was well past sixty and still beautiful in an old-fashioned way. Her silvery hair was elegantly coiffed, and Chuck thought to himself that the old cliche "not a hair out of place" could have been coined about her. Her elegant maroon dress was understated and expensive, and her white gloves spotless.

"Thank you, Mother," Chuck said. "You look as beautiful as ever."

Gladys smiled her tight little smile. "Thank you, Charles."

"And, Grandma, you look just great," Chuck said as he sat down on the edge of the couch next to his tiny, wrinkled grandmother.

"You're a damned liar and you know it, Chuck," the little woman replied, and cackled. "I look like a dried-up old prune."

Chuck's mother sucked in her breath. "Must you swear, Mother Goodall?" she asked.

"Why in hell shouldn't I swear?" Celeste Goodall shot back. "You've had forty years to get used to it."

Gladys's lips pursed into a tight line but she did not reply.

"Uh, I like your dress, Grandma," Chuck said quickly, hoping to forestall any more comments from Celeste. Celeste was wearing a deep blue knit that was covered with shiny sequins. Chuck could imagine what his mother's reaction had been to the dress.

"Mother has always had—well, different taste," Benson Goodall said as he entered the living room from the guest room.

"Do we have time for a drink?" Celeste asked.

Chuck checked his watch. "I think so," he said. "We're supposed to pick Faye up at seven." He ignored his parents' disapproving expressions and made himself and his grandmother weak drinks.

"So tell me about the young lady," Gladys said as she sat down in a plush chair. "I swear, Charles, now that Julie's gone. I wish you would get rid of this dreadful modern stuff and buy more—well, substantial furniture."

"I like the furnishings just fine," Chuck said mildly, not bothering to add that he had just bought the offending chair last week.

"Maybe he doesn't want the place to look like a mausoleum," Celeste observed.

Gladys sniffed a little and went on. "Do you work with the woman?"

"Her name is Faye, and, yes, I work with her," Chuck said. "She's our new tax manager." He handed a Scotch and soda to his grandmother and sipped his own. "She's a lovely woman."

"I'm sure she is," Gladys said approvingly.

"Sounds like a bore," Celeste said to no one in particular.

Chuck thought of Fatima and nearly choked on his drink. "No, Grandma, I can assure you that she's not a bore."

"A fellow accountant? Sounds good, son," Benson said approvingly as he sat down on a low-slung settee, gingerly stretching his legs out in front of him. "Nice, steady woman?"

"Not like poor Julie, dear?" his mother added.

"Not at all," Chuck assured them. At least she isn't most of the time, he added to himself.

Gladys looked relieved. "Hadn't we better get on our way?" she asked. "It wouldn't do to be late."

Chuck nodded and set his drink on the coffee table. So here goes, he thought as they all trooped out to his father's white Lincoln. They're all set to like Faye. *I just hope she can find something to like about them!*

Faye was putting the finishing touches to her makeup when the doorbell rang. "Coming!" she called, then picked up her evening purse and hurried to the front door. It wouldn't do to keep Chuck's family waiting!

She opened the door and smiled warmly at Chuck, who stared for a moment at the vision of beauty in front of him. "You look marvelous," he whispered as he took in her purple off-the-shoulder sheath and the way her thick dark hair cascaded down her back.

"Thank you," Faye said as her heart turned over at his crooked smile. "Where are we going to eat?"

"Dad and Mother like to eat downtown," Chuck said. "We eat there every time they come to town."

Gladys Goodall's mouth fell open as the dark-haired beauty in the revealing cocktail dress stepped outside. "I

106

thought he said she was an accountant," Gladys murmured.

"Well, there's no law that says she can't be beautiful too," Benson said thoughtfully as the woman took Chuck's arm. Celeste said nothing, but a knowing smile spread across her face as Chuck and the woman crossed the lawn and opened the back door of the car. Faye got in first and scooted to the middle of the seat. Chuck got in and closed the door.

"Mother, Dad, Grandmother, this is Faye Catalini," Chuck said. "Faye, my parents, Benson and Gladys Goodall, and my grandmother."

"Call me Celeste, everyone does," Celeste spoke up.

"Yes, ma'am, I will," Faye said, extending her hand to Gladys, who gripped it limply with her gloved hand before Benson shook it firmly. "I'm glad to meet both of you."

"Likewise," Benson said, trying hard not to stare at the expanse of creamy flesh revealed by Faye's dress. Gladys stared from Faye to her husband and her lips tightened. Uh-oh, Mama doesn't like skin showing, Faye thought as she stifled a smile at Gladys's modest though elegant dress. And those gloves! Faye hadn't seen anybody in a pair of gloves in years.

"Charles said you were an accountant," Gladys said as Benson backed out of the driveway.

"Yes, ma'am, I'm with the same firm that Chuck's with," Faye replied easily. "I've only been there for about a month."

"And in that time she's caught me in a couple of big bloopers," Chuck said. "She's good at her job."

Gladys's lips loosened a fraction. "I'm sure Mr. Wilson was pleased to find you," she said.

"Actually, Ray Donovan recommended me," Faye said. "Do you know Ray?"

"Isn't that the young man who put the liquor in the punch at Charles and Julie's rehearsal dinner?" Gladys asked a bit distastefully.

Chuck chuckled under his breath. "One and the same," he said.

Celeste laughed out loud. "Yes, that young man certainly livened up that party! You should have seen the look on Reverend Michaels's face when he took a gulp of that! Of course, I thought that particular bowl of punch was the best punch I'd had all year!"

Benson sniffed. "I have never quite seen the humor in the situation," he said. "Reverend Michaels was quite offended."

"Knowing Ray, you better be glad it was just at the rehearsal dinner and not the wedding reception," Chuck murmured.

"Well, to this day I wonder how that young man has managed to go as far as he has in the world," Gladys said.

"Talent and hard work," Faye said. "He's another person entirely at the office." At least he is most of the time, she thought to herself.

"Tell me, does the young man still love to play a joke?" Celeste asked. "I used to love it when he came home for the weekend with Chuck! We never knew what he was going to be up to next."

Chuck and Faye looked at each other and grinned. "Yes, Ray can still pull a fast one every so often," Chuck agreed.

Then Benson asked Chuck about a new condominium complex that was going up, and Faye settled back and listened as the conversation swirled around her. She hoped that the Goodalls were not as stuffy as they seemed, but she was afraid they were. I didn't realize people like this still existed, she thought as Gladys admonished Chuck for using a mild swear word. I thought they had gone out of style thirty years ago! She tried not to laugh at the look on Gladys's face when they drove by an adult movie theatre. Good grief, what would they think of Fatima? she wondered.

But Celeste was different. Once or twice Faye caught the little old lady's eye and found amusement there, the same amusement that she knew lurked in her own. Celeste sensed that Faye was a kindred soul too. Faye glanced over at Chuck and found him looking distinctly uncomfortable. He's caught in the middle, she thought sympathetically, and vowed to keep her amusement at his stuffy parents private.

She was not surprised that the restaurant chosen by Chuck's parents was the dining room in one of the stately old downtown hotels. As Gladys took Benson's arm, Faye wondered what their reaction would be to her favorite restaurant, a swinging steak house where the waiters wore costumes and the disco next door provided the background music. She stepped aside to let Chuck take his grandmother's arm, and Chuck extended his other arm to Faye.

"I just can't pass up the opportunity to have a beautiful woman on each arm," he said gallantly as he walked slowly up the steps to the lobby.

"Mrs. Good—Celeste, I just love your dress," Faye said as they entered the lobby.

"Well, thank you, dear," Celeste said loudly. "Gladys said it was dreadful when I picked it out, but I'll be damned if I'm going to dress all the time like I'm going to a funeral." Faye saw Gladys stiffen. "By the way, that dress of yours is lovely too. Did you get it at Sakowitz?"

"No, ma'am, Neiman's," Faye said.

"That's where mother does most of her shopping," Chuck explained.

"I love your dress, too, Mrs. Goodall," Faye said as they approached the dining room. Gladys Goodall might be hopelessly stuffy, Faye thought, but she had impeccable taste.

Gladys looked at Faye as though she hadn't taken the compliment seriously. "Why, thank you," she said. "I do like Neiman's."

The headwaiter immediately escorted them to a table at the edge of the room, out of the main traffic area. They were just about to sit down when a plump matron at the table next to theirs put her hand over her mouth, then called out. "Fatima! How are you, dear?"

Chuck's eyes flew open and Faye froze. Who on earth? She turned around slowly, praying for the floor to open and swallow her, and spotted the wife of a prominent heart surgeon. Fatima had danced for his last birthday party, and since the party had been held at their country cottage, Faye had driven out in her street clothes and put her costume on there, so Mrs. Rogers could easily recognize her tonight.

Please, please don't say anything about the dancing, Faye prayed as she extended her hand. "Mrs. Rogers, how are you?" she asked.

"Oh, I'm fine, just fine," Mrs. Rogers gushed as she gripped Faye's hand. "Fatima, we never had a chance to tell you just how much we enjoyed your dancing that night," she went on. "I swear, Horace accused me of trying to drum him up some more business by having you dance for his old cronies! Dear me, the way you wiggle is enough to give some of the poor old dears a coronary!"

110

"Uh, thank you, Mrs. Rogers," Faye said as she tried to ease away from Mrs. Rogers's tenacious grip—and her big mouth, she thought. Faye was afraid to turn around and see the expression on Chuck's parents' faces. But it would be worse, she realized, if Mrs. Rogers came out and said just what kind of dancing Fatima did. "If you'll excuse me—"

"Just let me introduce you to my friends," Mrs. Rogers said. "Fred, Eunice, this is Fatima. She's a belly dancer, and she has to be one of the best!"

"A belly dancer, huh?" Fred said loudly. "Dearie, would you like to dance for my brother's birthday party next month?"

Well, the cat was out of the bag now, Faye thought as she peeked around at Chuck's parents. Gladys was riveted to the floor with shock, and Benson was staring at her as though she had sprouted a second head. Chuck looked like a man who had been caught skinny-dipping in broad daylight.

Groaning inwardly, Faye got out her wallet and handed the man one of her cards. "Call me next week and we'll set up a time," she said, then turned to Chuck and his family. "I—I have a little part-time job," she stammered as Chuck pulled out the chair for his grandmother.

Benson pulled out Gladys's chair and she sank into it. "As a belly dancer?" she asked weakly.

"Yes," Faye said, and sat down in the chair Chuck pulled out for her.

Benson opened his mouth to speak but Celeste piped up first. "Oh, how *interesting*," she said as Chuck sat down beside her. "Tell me, do you get to dance often?"

If the question had come from Gladys or Benson, Faye would have changed the subject, but she felt she couldn't

111

be rude to her only ally at the table. "Yes, I dance two or three times a week."

"It's really quite a beautiful dance," Chuck said quickly.

Gladys swallowed. "But, dear, doesn't the firm pay you well? I mean, do you *have* to go do—well, uh, dance?"

"I don't do it for the money," Faye said softly. "I like to dance, Mrs. Goodall."

"I know what you mean," Celeste said as she opened her menu. "I didn't need Jean Claude's fees either. I did it because I wanted to."

"Wanted to do what, Grandma?" Chuck asked quickly. Let's get this conversation off of Fatima right now! he thought.

"I used to pose for him," Celeste said. "Jean Claude de Mist. He never made it big, but a few of his portraits are in the local museum."

Benson's eyes flew open and Gladys's mouth formed a little *O.* "You mean J. C. de Mist?" Benson choked.

"Yes, dear," Celeste said blithely. "That redheaded nude at the top of the gallery stairs is me. I posed for three others that were sold to private collectors."

Gladys looks as if she just swallowed a fork, Faye thought as she bit her lip to keep from laughing out loud. Benson looked thoroughly shocked, and Chuck stared at his grandmother incredulously. "I didn't know that, Grandma," he said.

"Neither did I," Benson murmured.

"I never said too much because it embarrassed the life out of your father, the poor dear," Celeste said. "Poor George! He never could go into that museum without blushing."

"You must have been very beautiful," Faye murmured,

112

searching Celeste's face and finding the remnants of what once must have been considerable beauty.

"Jean Claude thought so," Celeste said. "He moved out of town right after he did the big picture in the museum. I heard once he moved to Boston. Gladys, do you remember hearing of a J. C. de Mist when you were growing up?"

"No, Mother Goodall," Gladys murmured into her menu. "There wasn't much call for nu— I mean, those paintings in Boston."

"Oh, that's right," Celeste said. "Maybe it was New York. Greenwich Village. It was about 1925, I think, when he painted me. That was certainly an exciting era to come of age in."

"I'm sure it was," Faye said. "Did you really ride in rumble seats back then?"

Celeste was more than glad to respond to that question and others like it, and she managed to keep them entertained throughout a delicious roast beef dinner. Benson and Gladys contributed an occasional monosyllable—Faye feared that the twin shocks of her being a belly dancer and Celeste being a nude model had robbed them of most of their speech. Chuck seemed amused by his grandmother's stories, but uncomfortable at the same time. Was he embarrassed that his parents had found out about her dancing? Faye wondered.

Celeste finished her last bite of dessert and stood up. "Faye, would you mind seeing an old lady to the ladies' room?" she asked. "No, no, Gladys, don't you get up. I'm sure Faye won't mind taking me, and I know you and Benson would appreciate a few minutes alone with Chuck."

I bet they would, too, Faye thought as she stood up and took Celeste's arm. She sensed there was more to Celeste leaving Chuck to the mercy of his parents than a simple desire to visit the rest room. She glanced back as she and Celeste left the dining room, and saw Gladys watching them leave, her expression disapproving. "I have a feeling I'm the after-dinner mint," Faye said as she pushed open the door to the ladies' room.

"I wouldn't worry about it," Celeste said blithely as she detached herself from Faye's arm. "I doubt that she'll say anything to him about you, after that little bombshell I let loose."

"You did that on purpose?" Faye asked, getting a brush out of her purse.

"Of course," Celeste said as she washed her hands at the sink. "You don't think I would let out a sixty-year-old secret just because I'm getting senile, do you?"

Faye laughed. "I just *loved* the look on Chuck's mother's face when she realized which painting was you. You couldn't have shocked her more if you had walked in here naked tonight."

"Or if you had come in dancing," Celeste snickered. "Tell me, do you really get into it?"

"You bet, Celeste," Faye assured her, then her face sobered. "Chuck didn't take too well to it at first. In fact, I'm not sure he's used to it yet."

Celeste sobered also. "Don't give up on him, Faye," she said as she laid her hand on Faye's arm. "My son and his wife—they're good people, as good as they come, and they love Chuck a lot. But they're prim and stuffy and they raised him to be the same way. He needs somebody to help him loosen up a little. And, Faye, a woman like you might be able to help him do it."

"But what about his first wife?" Faye asked. "Or was she like that too?"

"No, Julie wasn't prim and stuffy, but then all *she* ever did was poke fun at him for being the way he was. She never did anything to help him change. But you would, Faye. Look, I'm just a meddlesome old grandmother and I realize that you and Chuck hardly know each other, but give it a try with him, Faye. See if you can get him to loosen up, just a little."

"I will," Faye promised as she took Celeste's arm to walk with her back to the table.

Spotting Chuck's square frame, Faye's heart flopped in her chest. No, she thought, remembering how Chuck had kissed her on several memorable occasions, he isn't *always* uptight and inhibited! She knew that once in a while Chuck's armor cracked, revealing the sensual man bound up deep inside him. It was a shame that he couldn't let that man loose more often, Faye thought, and wondered as she approached him how she could reach the warm, sensual man she knew was there.

CHAPTER SIX

Faye pushed back her chair and stood up. "That was a delicious dinner," she said. "I haven't had that good a steak in a long time."

Chuck laughed. "Yes, and this is the first time I've been waited on by Mr. T," he said, leaving a generous tip for the college-student waiter who had impersonated the popular television star.

They had dined at Faye's favorite restaurant, but since it was after ten and they had to work the next day, they decided to skip the disco next door and go straight home.

"Yes, Mr. T was cute, but I liked the Fonz better," Faye said as Chuck escorted her across the floor. "He graduated from college last year and quit this job."

"What a super way to put yourself through school," Chuck said, holding the door for her then following her out of the restaurant. "I was lucky that I didn't have to work," he added. "Mother and Dad paid for it all."

At the mention of his parents, Faye glanced at Chuck. "Uh, did your mother and father say anything to you about me?" she asked hesitantly.

Chuck laughed out loud. "No, not a single solitary word," he said. "But Grandma wrote and said that her portrait had been moved to one of the back rooms of the museum. My mother just happens to be on the board of directors."

"Oh, what a shame," Faye said, and she laughed with Chuck.

"Not really. It was a terrible portrait," Chuck said dryly. "It was one of those horrible impressionistic things. As far as I'm concerned, if you're going to paint a nude, at least paint it so you can really see it!" Faye laughed, and when Chuck realized what he'd said, he blushed a brilliant shade of red. "Well, I didn't mean— Oh, you know—"

"I agree," Faye sputtered. "By all means, get those sexy little details in focus!"

Chuck laughed at his own embarrassment. "Do you know that I'm thirty-five and I still hide my *Playboy* magazines under the bed? Julie used to tease me about that. She used to tease me about a lot of things, come to think of it. Well, that's water under the bridge. Come on, I better get you home. We've got that meeting with the Galleria bigwigs in the morning."

"That's the trouble with dating a colleague," Faye groused as Chuck unlocked the car door. "You always know when I have something important in the morning!"

Chuck got in on his side and shut the door. "Just making sure Cox and Wilson gets its money's worth out of us," he teased as he started the engine. "Tomorrow's Friday. Are you dancing?"

Faye nodded. "I have a seven o'clock performance, but I should be finished and home by nine. Is that too late for you?"

"Absolutely not," Chuck said. Especially for what I have in mind, he added to himself. "How about if I fix you dinner at my place?"

Faye nodded slowly. "Sounds lovely."

117

"Dress casually. I'll pick you up at nine," Chuck said, proud of himself for the nonchalant way he'd carried off his invitation.

They rode in silence toward Faye's house. As they pulled up in Faye's driveway and Chuck killed the engine, he offered to walk her to the door. Following her inside, he took her into his arms and kissed and caressed her with a passion that stole Faye's breath away. As she moaned and clung to him the passion spiraled between them, as it did every time he touched her. *More! More!* her body screamed as Chuck moved away.

"See you tomorrow night," he said, touching her face with trembling fingers.

Faye nodded and shut the door behind him, then wandered into the kitchen and poured Lenore a bowl of cat food. The little cat came and wound herself around Faye's feet. "I'm falling for him, Lenore," she said, picking up the cat and cuddling her. Lenore stuck out her tongue and licked her paw. "That's right, Lenore, I like him when he kisses me. Of course, I like him just as much when he's not kissing me."

She put the cat down and headed for her bedroom. After showering and pulling on a slinky black teddy, she turned back the covers on her bed and picked up the papers on the Galleria accounts, intending to go over them once more before she went to sleep. But as she stared at the figures, her mind kept wandering away from the important account to Chuck.

He was kind, he was funny, he was a marvelous companion, she thought, and his kisses could turn her bones to water. At first that had been enough, but in the past month her desire for Chuck had grown to the point of wanting more. They had grown mentally and emotionally closer,

118

she mused. Wasn't it time that their closeness extended to the physical part of their relationship?

Faye frowned at the papers in her lap as she tried to make sense out of the numbers, then she became annoyed with herself and put the papers back in her briefcase. She didn't like Chuck *just* physically, she thought, but she did like him that way, too, and wanted to become his lover.

But that move must come from him, Faye told herself. She could make her desire known in subtle ways, but when it came right down to it, he would have to make the first move. If she made the first move, she reflected, it would set a pattern for their relationship, and she didn't want that.

Chuck unloaded the sack of groceries and put the thick T-bone steaks in the refrigerator. Chuckie, old boy, tomorrow night's the night, he thought as he unloaded a head of lettuce and an envelope of salad-dressing mix. He put the lettuce in the refrigerator and the dressing mix in the cabinet. He was going to feed her steak and mellow her with wine, he mused, and she was going to float into his arms and stay there until morning. He removed tomatoes and two big baking potatoes from the grocery bag, put them into the refrigerator, then found a bottle of good red wine under the kitchen sink and put that in to chill overnight. Everything had to be perfect tomorrow, he thought.

After turning out the kitchen light, Chuck headed for his bedroom. He showered quickly, pulled on his pajama bottoms, and climbed into bed. He would have to be sure and remember not to wear pajama bottoms tomorrow night, he told himself.

Chuck got out the papers he was supposed to study for his morning meeting and stared at the figures, but couldn't stop the silly grin that creased his mouth. He was going to seduce Faye tomorrow night! He was going to wine her and dine her and then make love to her until morning! Not that he would have any trouble with that third part, he thought, if the signals Faye had been sending him were any indication. She was subtle, but he could see the desire in her eyes when she looked at him, and she knew that his eyes sent the same message to her.

"Tomorrow, Faye," he whispered aloud. "Tomorrow night I'll make you mine."

Chuck ran up the steps to his house and jabbed the key in the lock. Of all nights for Mr. Wilson to ask him to work late! It was after eight, and he was supposed to pick Faye up at nine. He'd wanted to have everything done—the table set, the candles out, the steaks marinating in his favorite sauce. Now he wouldn't have time to do half of what he'd wanted to do. And he wasn't about to call Faye and postpone the date, for even thirty minutes; he wanted the evening to be perfect.

He tore the tie out from around his neck and quickly draped his suit back on the hanger. Oh, well, at least he'd managed to cover for Faye so she could make her dancing appointment, he thought. Old man Wilson had wanted her to stay late, too, but Chuck's quick thinking when he saw the panic in her eyes had resulted in Mr. Wilson's letting her go early. Chuck frowned. Unfortunately, it had meant he had to stay that much later.

After stripping and showering as quickly as he could, Chuck blew his hair dry as he stood naked in front of the mirror. He glanced at his lean body. Would Faye find him physically appealing, or did her taste run to a bigger, bulkier man? he wondered. Then he pulled on a pair of jeans and a knit top, grabbed his dirty clothes and dumped them in the washer.

He checked the clock on the stove and swore when he saw it read 8:37. He jerked open the cabinet where Julie used to keep the tablecloths, realized Julie had taken them with her when she'd left, and rummaged around for replacements. The best he could do was a couple of old rattan placemats that looked all right but were hardly romantic. He slapped them down on the table and spent precious minutes looking for the candle holders, finally unearthing a strange-smelling candle in a blue globe. Any candlelight was better than none, he figured, and put the candle in the middle of the table.

Chuck put his everyday pottery and stainless steel knives and forks down on the placemats, wishing he had had enough time to polish his mother's old sterling flatware, even if it would have looked funny with the placemats. He started to take the steaks out of the refrigerator to marinate, then realized he had to leave if he was going to make it to Faye's on time. As he hurried out the front door, a tremor of nervousness passed through him. What was he doing tonight? he wondered. What would Faye think?

Chuck tried to put his nerves firmly out of his mind, but they kept returning to haunt him on the short drive to Faye's. What would she do when he asked her the big question? he thought. Would she melt into his arms, or would she laugh in his face? After all, it had been over ten years since he'd deliberately set out to seduce a woman. They might not do it the same way they used to, he mused. Oh, come on, Chuck, he chided himself. Go for it! After all, that's the only way you're going to get anywhere with her.

Faye had just stepped into her new sandals when the doorbell rang. He's never a moment late, she thought as she picked up her purse and headed for the front door. She opened the door and smiled. "Hi," she said softly.

"Hi, yourself," Chuck replied, leaning down to plant a tender kiss on her lips. "Ready to go?"

Faye nodded. "Thanks for covering for me, by the way," she said as Chuck opened the car door for her. "Did it make you late?"

"Oh, not really," Chuck lied, and got into the car. "How was your performance?"

"Well, I might have sent a couple of the older ones to the hospital with high blood pressure, but most of them loved it."

"Better be careful, you might send somebody to the nursing home sometime," Chuck teased.

"I *was* at the nursing home," Faye said dryly. "No, really," she protested when Chuck laughed. "They hired me for the director's birthday. One old man followed me all the way to the door in his wheelchair. I had to promise him I'd come back for his birthday before he'd let me go home!"

"And you'll go, of course," Chuck said.

"Of course I will," Faye replied softly. "You should have seen the way their faces lit up."

"That's good," Chuck said, reaching out to pat Faye's hand.

Maybe he's getting used to the dancing, Faye thought as Chuck drove. Maybe he's getting used to both sides of my nature. His parents' open disapproval hadn't seemed to discourage him, and he was beginning to ask about her dancing. Lost in thought, she didn't notice until they were

122

almost at Chuck's house that he'd been silent, and seemed distracted. She sensed his nervousness as he pulled into the driveway of a modern-looking house and killed the engine.

"We're here," he said, opening his door.

Get a grip on yourself! Chuck admonished himself as he got out of the car and opened Faye's door. He felt as nervous as a college freshman at his first big love scene. But you haven't seduced a woman in years, a nasty little inner voice taunted him, and you weren't very good at it back then.

Together, they walked to his front door, Chuck opening it and moving aside to let Faye enter. "Your home is lovely," she murmured as Chuck shut the door behind them.

"Thank you. I bought a few pieces to fill in when Julie took some of the furniture," Chuck said. "Can I get you a drink?"

"Sure," Faye said, and followed across the living room and into the kitchen.

"What would you like?" Chuck asked, opening the cabinet where he kept his liquor.

"That Scotch looks interesting," Faye said. Chuck poured her a weak Scotch and soda and himself a stronger one, draining it in two gulps.

"Ah, that's better," he said, and took the steaks and baking potatoes out of the refrigerator.

Faye carried her drink into the dining room. Chuck picked up one of the potatoes and placed it on the aluminum baking frame Julie had sworn by. He'd originally planned to bake the potatoes slowly in the oven, but tonight there had been no time for that.

"Chuck? Was this your mother's silver tray?" Faye asked.

"Yes, it was," Chuck called out as he placed the second potato on the frame. He opened the door of the microwave and put the potatoes inside.

"No, Chuck!" Faye cried as she saw what he'd done, but she couldn't get across the floor before Chuck had turned on the microwave timer.

The inside of the microwave lit up, sparks flying from the sides of the oven to the aluminum baking rod. Chuck whirled around, but before he could shut off the oven it flashed brightly once and went dark.

Chuck stared for a moment at the dark microwave. "What have I done?" he asked.

Faye grasped the cord by the rubber handle and pulled the plug out of the wall. "There. I don't quite trust these things when they're still plugged in."

Chuck pushed open the microwave and with a pot holder withdrew the melted tangle of aluminum frame and potato. "I forgot not to put it in there," he said as he dumped the mess in the sink.

"No harm done," Faye said brightly. "Except to the microwave, of course. Sorry about that."

Chuck nodded nervously. "I guess you're right. I don't have any more potatoes."

"That's all right, I'm sure the steaks will be enough," Faye said, and sipped her drink. What on earth was the matter with Chuck tonight? she wondered. He seemed nervous and jumpy. And the mistake with the potato frame— he had to be really rattled to do a thing like that.

"I guess I can just make a little more salad," Chuck said.

He flavored the steaks and put them under the broiler, got out the tomatoes and lettuce, and with slightly unsteady fingers, chopped them and put them into a big salad bowl. Then he took out the little envelope of dressing, groaning when he read the list of ingredients because he didn't have any vinegar with which to make it. Sighing, he reached into the refrigerator and withdrew a bottle of Thousand Island. "Is this all right?" he asked.

Faye nodded, wondering what happened to the envelope. "Sure, that's fine," she said.

Chuck poured too much dressing on both salads, brought them into the dining room, and returned to the kitchen. "Would you like to eat the salad as a first course?" he asked, picking up a box of matches. "The steaks should be ready in a moment. Oh, would you like to have wine with dinner?" he asked, and opened the refrigerator, then held up a bottle.

"Sure," Faye said. She picked up the two wineglasses on the counter, followed Chuck into the dining room, and sat down on one of the dining room chairs.

Chuck lit the strange-looking candle in the middle of the table, and took the foil off the wine bottle. He withdrew his pocketknife and folded out a small corkscrew. "Julie took the good one when she left," he said as he screwed the corkscrew into the cork.

Chuck pulled on the cork, but it only moved the barest fraction of an inch. He pulled harder, but the stubborn cork remained firmly in place. Determined to dislodge it, Chuck gave a vicious yank and the cork suddenly pulled free. Chuck's hand slipped and the bottle slipped sideways in his hand, liberally dousing Faye with the expensive red wine. She squealed as she jumped up out of the chair.

"Oh, Faye, I'm *sorry*," Chuck said, jerking the nearly empty bottle upright, splashing more wine on both of them. "Oh, I'm so *sorry!*"

"No harm done," Faye said, trying not to laugh in

125

Chuck's face. What was wrong with him tonight? she wondered. He hadn't done anything right! "I won't melt," she added.

"Oh, Faye, I got it all over you," Chuck said, and started wiping her face and her neck with a handkerchief he'd pulled from his pocket.

"You didn't get my jeans, just my hair and my blouse," she said.

"Look, you go wash this stuff off and I'll clean up in here," Chuck said. "Here, let me show you to the bathroom."

On the way to the bathroom he led her down the hall past the master bedroom. Faye admired the masculine room done in creams and browns and a bathroom done in similar colors. Chuck opened a cabinet and pulled out a couple of fluffy towels and a washcloth.

"Here, you can use these to get cleaned up, and I'll leave a shirt out on the bed for you to put on. And, Faye, I'm sorry, I really am."

"Hey, that's all right," Faye said. She reached out and licked her lips. "Good wine."

Chuck reached out and kissed her wine-drenched lips. "Good wine. Very good wine," he said approvingly as he moved to take her into his arms. Faye swayed toward him, ready for the kiss and caress that was bound to follow, when she stopped and wrinkled her nose. "What's that I smell?" she asked. "It smells like something's burning."

My steaks! Chuck cried in anguish.

He was out of the bathroom and down the hall at a run, Faye at his heels. Chuck opened the oven door and choked as a billowing cloud of smoke rose up and engulfed him. Coughing and choking, he pulled the broiler from the oven and ran it to the sink, where two hopelessly burned steaks toppled down beside the melted potato frame.

"That does it, I give up," Chuck said dispiritedly, and threw a pot holder down in the sink. He walked into the living room, extinguishing the strange-smelling candle in the dining room that was even overpowering the smell of smoke from the kitchen. He pulled off his glasses and wiped the greasy smoke from the lenses.

Faye followed Chuck out to the living room and sat down beside him on the couch. "What are you giving up on?" she asked softly. "Everybody has a bum night in the kitchen now and then." Chuck shrugged and looked down at his hands in his lap. "Come on, tell me. It isn't just dinner, is it?"

Chuck shook his head. "No, if I had just been fixing dinner none of this would have happened. I wasn't just trying to cook for you, I was trying to seduce you." He looked up at Faye, misery written all over his slightly smoky face. "I wanted to take you to bed with me tonight. I tried to do it right—you know, candles and wine and a good meal. Then I got home late and I couldn't find a tablecloth, and that candle stinks and I ruined everything." He looked down into his lap again. "I'm sorry, Faye. I wanted it to be nice for a special person like you."

Faye got up off the couch and knelt between Chuck's knees. "Do you have any idea how incredibly sweet you are?" she asked. "To plan a special evening for me? But you don't have to seduce me, you know. All you have to do is ask."

Chuck raised his eyes and met hers. "Do you mean that?" he asked.

Faye nodded. "All this is nice, but you don't have to impress me, Chuck. This isn't you." She reached out and stroked his cheek. "Just be yourself. That will be more than enough for me."

Chuck leaned down and captured Faye's mouth in a long, lingering kiss. The taste of the wine on her lips and the smoke on his mingled together. Finally, Chuck pulled away and put his hands on her shoulders. "Faye, will you let me make love to you tonight?" he asked.

Faye nodded. "I would be delighted for you to make love to me." She kissed him once again, then stood and pulled him up with her. "But you have to feed me first."

Chuck winced. "There isn't much left in the refrigerator," he said.

"How about take-out chicken?" Faye asked. "I'll clean up in the kitchen while you go pick it up."

Chuck leaned down and planted a kiss on Faye's cheek. "You're something else," he said, then released her and walked to the front door. Faye waited until she heard his car start to let out a whoop of laughter. Then she walked into the kitchen and started cleaning up.

She'd just wiped up the last of the mess when Chuck returned carrying a box of fried chicken and a sack of French fries. "Say, were the salads still edible?" he asked as he sat the box of chicken between the place settings at the dining room table.

"Not really, once they got flavored by that candle you had out there," Faye said, bringing two cans of soda.

Chuck took one from her and drank deeply, then sniffed the air. "How did you get rid of that horrible smell?" he asked.

"Opened the windows and burned a match in here where the candle smell was the strongest," Faye said as she sat down at the table. "Now I smell like burning matches and red wine."

128

Chuck sniffed his arm as he sat down. "And I smell like burned beef." He opened the box of chicken and handed Faye a packet of fries from the sack. "So much for steaks and wine!"

"At this point I would settle for a peanut butter sandwich," Faye said, picking out three drumsticks and putting them on her plate. "I'm starved!"

Chuck poked around in the box, then picked up a thigh and slipped it onto Faye's plate, quickly taking one of her drumsticks. "You got 'em all," he explained when Faye stared down pointedly at the thigh. He then found a piece of white meat and took a bite out of it. "You know, now that I know that you want me, I'm not even nervous."

Faye swallowed a bite of chicken and nodded. "It's amazing what a little bit of reassurance will do," she said between bites. And I wish I had a little myself, she thought as they ate in silence.

Faye had been intimate with a couple of special men in the past. They had always seemed pleased enough with her and she had always enjoyed the experience, but she'd always come away from the intimacy with a disappointing feeling, thinking, Is this all there is? It had always puzzled her because she knew she wasn't inhibited about sex. She'd enjoyed it but it had never been the earth-shattering experience for her that she supposed it to be.

What was it going to be like with Chuck? she wondered. Now that he had taken the initiative and said he wanted to be her lover, she was beginning to have second thoughts. Would he be as prim and shy in bed as he was out of it? Would she be disappointed by his lovemaking?

Faye started in on a second piece of chicken and pushed her doubts to the back of her mind. She would take this relationship for whatever it was, she decided, even if it wasn't that great at first. Maybe she could help Chuck loosen up later, she thought, if he needed to. After all, he didn't have Superman hiding behind his horn-rimmed glasses, and it wouldn't be fair to expect him to turn into an aggressive, macho lover in bed. Besides, his kisses and caresses had certainly been delightful. Maybe the rest would be too.

Chuck finished the last of his chicken. "Did you get enough to eat?" he asked as Faye licked the crumbs from her fingers.

"Yes, and it was delicious." She picked up the plates and dumped the chicken bones into the empty box. "Let's get this cleaned up so we don't have to face it in the morning."

Chuck stood up and smiled down at Faye's slightly grubby face. "You will stay the night, then?" he asked. "I wasn't sure you would want to."

Faye nodded. "Do you suppose you could run my clothes through the washer sometime? I hate to go home smelling like an old winery."

Chuck nodded. "Tell you what. Go in my bathroom and take off your clothes and hand them out the door to me. I'll put them in to wash while you get that wine washed off."

Faye stood tiptoe and planted a kiss in the middle of Chuck's lips. "I have a better idea. Why don't you join me after you've put the clothes in the wash? We'll conserve water."

"Sounds good to me," he said as he grabbed her hand and led her back down the hall toward his bathroom.

Faye ducked in and quickly stripped, opening the door just a crack and thrusting the clothes out to Chuck. A bath together would be nice, she thought as she poked around the bathroom. Scented soap, maybe? She opened one cabinet and found only linens, but in the second cabinet she found a bottle of old-fashioned bubble bath, picked it up and looked at it.

Had it belonged to his former wife? she wondered. The last thing she wanted to smell like was his ex-wife! She opened the bottle, sniffed, and detected the faintly spicy fragrance that Celeste had worn. *Thank you, Celeste!* Faye thought as she turned on the tap. She showered first, washing the wine out of her hair with some of Chuck's shampoo, then poured a little of the bubble bath into the water as she filled the tub.

Faye had just turned off the tap when Chuck walked into the bathroom, naked as the day he was born except for his glasses. Faye stared wordlessly at the hard, fit body that had always been hidden beneath his clothes. She'd known he was fit, but she had not realized that Chuck's body was the epitome of masculine perfection, or at least that he was *her* epitome of masculine perfection. His shoulders were broad and firmly muscled without being bulky, and his muscular chest tapered to a trim, flat waist. Allowing her gaze to drift lower, Faye stared at the strength of his hips and thighs. Chuck was gorgeous, she thought, absolutely gorgeous. Looking back up, she found that Chuck was blushing furiously at her intimate inspection.

"I'm sorry for staring," she said hoarsely. "It's just that you're so perfect."

Chuck shook his head as he reached out and ran his hand down her arm, lightly touching the side of her breast. "I'm not the one who's perfect," he said as his eyes eagerly gazed at her high, firm breasts and light brown nipples. He touched the tip of one of her nipples with the pad of his finger and watched as it contracted into a hard little knot

131

of desire. He let his gaze wander lower, past her supple midriff and the firm, tight waist he remembered from her costume, then took in the sexy, softly rounded stomach that had haunted his dreams for so many nights. Then his eyes drifted lower, to the delights that he had to this point seen only in his imagination. He gazed at her gently rounded hips and her shapely thighs, and spotted a small birthmark on the top of her left thigh.

"Faye, I can't believe how beautiful you really are." The blush of embarrassment left his face and the flush of desire replaced it. "I want you so badly I hurt with it."

"I want you, too, Chuck," Faye said as she reached out and took him by the hand. "But I hate to waste this perfectly delightful tub of bubbles."

"Me either. Hey, do you mind if I shut that door? I love it when the bathroom gets all fogged up." He closed it gently, then sank down in the tub, the heat from the water immediately fogging his glasses.

Faye climbed into the water, too, sitting opposite Chuck in the frothing bubbles. Chuck dipped his glasses in the water, wiped them, and put them back on. "Why are you still wearing those things?" she asked.

"The better to see you with, my dear," he leered across the tub. "In fact, it's the only way to see you, my dear. I can't see you clearly that far away."

"Guess I'll have to fix that," Faye said as she scooted across the tub and nestled as close as she could get. She reached up and plucked the glasses off his nose. "Can you see me from here?" she asked.

"Sure, darlin', you're as clear as day," Chuck teased, sputtering when Faye hit him in the mouth with a wet washcloth. She, in turn, was treated to a wandering hand groping for her interesting parts under the water. "Umm,

132

that feels nice," Chuck murmured as his hand slid around the small of her waist and tickled lightly.

"Chuck, stop that, you're *tickling* me!" Faye squealed as his tormenting fingers found and teased the sensitive skin under her ribs. She tried to pull away and sloshed the water back and forth in the tub.

"I'm what?" Chuck teased as his questing fingers traveled up and found the underside of her breast.

"I said that you were, uh, ah, never mind," Faye moaned as Chuck's fingers found the tip of her breast under the surface of the water and moved back and forth over it.

When he felt her nipple hard and hot in his hand, he moved to the other breast and ministered to it similarly, drawing his fingers back and forth until Faye was trembling. Her own hands slid down Chuck's slick shoulders and found the hair-roughened chest that she so loved to touch. She caressed one of his flat masculine nipples until it was hard, then her fingers traveled over to the other one.

"I'll quit this if you will," she promised as she flicked her fingernails across the hardened nub, knowing he was enjoying it as much as she was.

Chuck turned Faye around so that they were facing in the same direction, and pulled her up against his chest. "Now, a man like me, who can't see the woman he's with, needs another method of getting to know her body. So we do it like this." He wrapped his arms around her and slowly started exploring her neck and shoulders with his fingers.

Faye moaned and tried to push away. "But I can't touch you like this," she protested.

Chuck pulled her back firmly against his chest. "No, you can't," he agreed. "But remember, I'm not just touching you. I'm getting to know you by touch so that blind old me will know sexy little you whenever I feel you." His hands drifted down from her shoulders to her breasts.

"You're not *that* blind!" Faye protested as his hands drew circles on her breasts and nipples.

"No, but we can pretend, can't we?"

Chuck laughed as his hands drifted lower, to the supple indentation of her waist. Faye shivered as his hands drew erotic patterns on the soft skin with the firm layer of muscle under it. Chuck pressed lightly on her stomach and found the expected tight muscles under her smooth flesh.

"You have the sexiest stomach I have ever seen," he said as his hand drifted lower and began a slow, sensuous massage of the already sensitive flesh he found there. Her senses coming alive, Faye moaned as his palm dipped lower and lower, creeping toward the warmth of her femininity.

"Do you like this?" Chuck asked as his hand caressed the soft skin of her inner thighs.

"Oh, yes!" Faye gasped as his hand found the warmth of her desire and stroked it lightly. Her senses suddenly erupting out of control, she arched and shuddered in his arms, tremors of delight shaking her body.

Chuck reached down and nuzzled the slick wet skin on her neck. "Did you like that?" he asked.

Faye nodded, then sat up as Chuck pushed lightly on her shoulders. She climbed out of the tub, wrapped one of the towels around her and looped the other one around Chuck's shoulders. Still trembling slightly with passion, she let him dry her flushed body with her towel, then he dried his quickly.

"Shall we continue?" he asked as he swept her into his

134

arms and carried her into the bedroom, where he laid her on the bed.

"Better watch out, you'll hurt yourself carrying me around," Faye protested as he lowered her body to the bed.

"You're not heavy," Chuck said, and slid onto the bed beside her, his lips capturing hers in a long, slow kiss.

"We haven't done much of this tonight, have we?" he asked, and nibbled her lower lip.

They kissed for long moments, then Chuck let his lips travel down the soft expanse of her shoulders and her breasts. Faye, who had thought her passion slaked for the evening, was surprised and delighted to feel desire curling within her again. Now that she was in a position to touch Chuck, she reached out and with eager fingers stroked the hard warmth of his arms and chest, then let her fingers drift lower, past the firmness of his waist to the strong masculinity of his hips. She could feel his desire for her, and this fueled her renewed passion for him. He touched her and kissed her and caressed her until they were both nearly out of their minds, then he parted her legs and with a bold sure stroke made them one.

Faye gasped as she felt his masculine power invade her body. Eagerly her hips arched up to his, wanting to feel every bit of his tender possession. Chuck waited for a moment, letting them both savor the reality of their coming together, then began to move, slowly at first and then faster, as Faye matched his movements. Kissing and caressing was for the moment forgotten as they savored the erotic union of their bodies. They moved together, thrusting and feinting and twisting back and forth, moans of pleasure tearing from the back of Faye's throat as the fine wire between them was drawn tighter. Chuck's face was knitted in a frown of concentration and pleasure as he fought to hold back his release until he was sure she'd had hers. Faye swirled higher and higher, then her body arched as waves of delight came crashing around her. As he felt her stiffen, Chuck gave in and let delight overtake him, too, tearing through his body as he shuddered above her.

Without pulling away, Chuck lay down on his side and turned Faye to face him. "Are you all right?" he asked softly.

Faye nodded and snuggled into his chest. "Yes, I'm all right," she whispered. Of course she was, she thought. She was better than all right. She had never responded to a man like this before! A part of her wanted to tell him, but another part was embarrassed to say it out loud, so Faye contented herself with kissing Chuck's chest.

"Give me a minute and we'll have another go at it," he said as he stroked the back of Faye's neck, missing the look of astonishment that passed across her face.

Later they made love a second time, Chuck again bringing Faye to the pinnacle of rapture and stunning her with the depths of her response to him. She laughed and she cried and moaned in his arms, Chuck bringing her pleasure she'd only dreamed about.

When they were finally spent, Chuck asleep in her arms, Faye allowed herself to smile in the dark with amusement at her earlier thoughts. So she hadn't expected to find Superman in her bed! Little did she know! Chuck had unlocked a door tonight and revealed a world of pleasure that she had not even known existed.

Faye snuggled closer to him and wrapped her arm around his waist. Did Chuck realize what delight he had brought her tonight? she wondered. Or had it always been that way for him? He was probably used to having a woman go crazy in his arms, she thought, so her response wouldn't have been anything special to him. Despite her dancing, Faye was actually shy about her own sexual responses, and too embarrassed to tell him just how special their lovemaking had been.

Chuck stared at the dawn-lightened ceiling and cradled the sleeping woman in his arms. Faye had turned over just a few minutes ago, the motion of her body waking Chuck out of a dream in which he was making love to her again. I'll give it about thirty minutes and I'll make that dream come true, he thought as he watched the early morning sunlight filter through the windowshades. He could hardly wait to have her come alive in his arms again.

Chuck frowned into the gray stillness as a thought crossed his mind. What man in Faye's past had awakened her to her sexuality? He must have been one hell of a lover to have taught her to have that kind of response! Or maybe it was just in her nature to be that passionate. Was she like that with everyone she made love with?

Chuck sighed and ran his hand down the warmth of Faye's shoulder as doubts assailed his ego. It was probably her nature to be sensual, he concluded. So how long could he keep a woman like Faye satisfied? He had been happy and satisfied last night, but had she? And if she had been satisfied last night, how long could he keep her that way? Would she remain content with him? he wondered. Or would she, like Julie, eventually need more than he could give?

CHAPTER SEVEN

"Are you looking forward to the weekend?" Chuck asked softly as he and Faye stepped into the elevator that would take them down to the parking garage.

Faye nodded as she reached down and squeezed his hand in the privacy of the elevator. "I can hardly wait!" she said eagerly. "I'm sorry we can't leave tonight, but I had already booked this dancing appointment three months ago and I would have hated to cancel. I don't want to get the reputation of being unreliable."

"I can understand that," Chuck said. He leaned over and planted a quick kiss on her parted lips. "Besides, since Monday is the Fourth of July, we'll have three days."

"I sure hope everybody goes out and gets sunburned like we're going to, or it's going to be obvious what we've been up to."

"Speak for yourself, paleface," Chuck teased. "I already have a tan, thank you."

The elevator ground to a halt and they stepped off. "Yeah, but you cheat and use a sunlamp," Faye griped. She'd been surprised when Chuck had started using it a couple of weeks ago on his pale skin. But he hadn't burned and was, in fact, developing a rich, dark tan. She'd been working on her tan during weekends, and with her natural olive complexion she, too, was turning brown.

"All's fair in love and war and the sunshine," Chuck quipped. He smiled his crooked grin and Faye could feel her heart turn over. "See you tomorrow, angel."

Faye got into the car and Chuck reached in and patted her shoulder. "See you in the morning," she said.

She braved the heavy evening traffic, made it home quickly, and began the painstaking process of making herself into Fatima. Three hours later, after she had danced for a most appreciative audience of farmers and ranchers, Faye stood at the bathroom mirror again and looked at the image of Fatima that stared back at her. I think Chuck's getting used to the idea of my dancing, she thought as she creamed off her makeup and stepped under the shower. It didn't seem to bother him anymore. *And I'm glad, because I'm falling for him—falling in a very big way.*

She washed the glitter out of her hair, quickly soaped and washed up, then wrapped herself in her old satin robe and hauled her suitcase out of the closet. She carefully folded and packed enough underwear for three days, then cut the tags off her new bikini and wrapped it into a little ball. It wasn't much more than a few strings and triangles, but South Padre was a sophisticated resort area and she was sure she wouldn't shock anyone with its brevity.

Faye packed the rest of her clothes for the trip, remembered the latest purchase she'd made, and pulled the new teddy out of a drawer. It was a soft pink. She held it up to her body and stared at herself in the mirror, thinking, I hope he likes it. Her eyes misted as she imagined Chuck pushing the narrow straps off her shoulders and loving her in the gentle, masterful way he'd been making love to her for the last month. I've fallen in love with him, she thought as she snapped the suitcase shut and sat down beside it on the bed.

Their lovemaking had been marvelous from the first, but her love for him was more than physical. Chuck was one of the most peaceful, restful people she'd ever been around, and she treasured the oasis of quiet that he brought to her hectic life. They went out a lot, but on many of the nights Faye was free, they ate dinner at her place and just spent a quiet evening together, talking. Although he hadn't gone to watch her dance again, Chuck was often waiting with a meal or a snack ready when Faye returned home from a performance.

Faye was happier than she had ever been in her life. Thanks to Chuck Goodall, she thought. *I hope he feels the same way about me.*

Chuck threw in his old boxer swim trunks and snapped his suitcase shut. He wished he'd found the time to go shopping for a new suit, but his department had just undertaken a new job, and between time spent at that and time with Faye, shopping had gone by the wayside. If it came to a choice between Faye or shopping, he thought, Faye won hands down!

He turned back the bed and checked his watch. Faye should be home from dancing by now, he thought. He started to call her to make sure she got home safely but decided not to bother her, since she was probably trying to pack. He'd wanted to drive her to her performance tonight, but still couldn't bring himself to watch her dance again. The idea of Faye's being Fatima the belly dancer was still hard for him to accept. I'm trying, he thought as he crawled under the covers.

But he knew that wasn't really what he was trying to get used to. It was what the dancing revealed about Faye that still bothered him. Now that he was her lover, he knew

140

intimately of her highly sensual nature, and that nature frightened him more than he cared to admit. Although she seemed quite happy with their relationship now, would he be able to continue to satisfy her? he wondered. Or would she need a more sensual man than he? Chuck turned out the light and turned onto his side. Although he tried to tell himself not to worry, that nagging doubt wouldn't quite go away.

Faye raised her nose out of the whodunit she was reading in the car and peered around at the lush green countryside. "Are we almost there?" she asked.

Chuck had picked her up at six thirty in the morning. Fortified with a thermos of coffee and a sack of doughnuts, they had set out. Chuck found a radio station that suited him, and Faye had become absorbed in one of the bestselling thrillers she'd promised herself to read for weeks now.

"Yes, we're almost at Harlingen," Chuck said. "We can go straight to Port Isabel and across the causeway, unless you'd rather go through Brownsville first."

Faye shook her head. "Why don't we drive over in the morning and go shopping in Matamoros for part of the day? I'm eager to hit the beach this afternoon."

"As you wish," Chuck agreed cheerfully.

Chuck whistled under his breath as they crossed the tall, wide causeway that would take them across to South Padre. When they pulled off the causeway and were on the long, narrow island, he said, "Did you realize this place was so built up?"

Faye shook her head. "It looks like a little Miami." She looked around with interest at the profusion of high-rises and condominiums that lined both sides of the road. "Hey, I'm going to like this."

"I thought it was going to be all rustic and romantic," Chuck said, trying to hide his disappointment.

Faye reached over and squeezed his hand. "Rustic, hardly. But we'll make it romantic, Chuck." She pointed to a high-rise hotel on the ocean side of the island. "I made our reservations there. They have a dining room on the top floor with entertainment and dancing."

Chuck pulled into the driveway of the hotel, and before long they were checked in and up in their room. "Do we want to swim in the pool or in the ocean?" Faye asked as she looked out the window and down at the beach and the pool, both of which were packed.

Chuck peered down and shrugged. "Let's try both," he said. He opened his suitcase and pulled out his swimsuit, and Faye got out her new suit. In a minute they'd changed. Chuck looked over at Faye's new suit and swallowed. "Uh, th-that's a nice suit," he stammered as he stared at the wide expanse of firm flesh it left uncovered.

Faye looked over at Chuck's modest suit and smiled. Although he was perfectly comfortable with his body around her, she could sense that he was still quite modest otherwise. She had known he'd be embarrassed the first time he saw her brief bikini, but thought that if he saw her free and uninhibited about her body, he might not be so prim about his own.

Chuck looked down at his own suit and grinned ruefully. "I guess mine's out of style," he said.

"You look just fine," Faye replied.

They locked their door behind them and took the elevator down to the lobby. Soon they had staked out a spot on the beach, near the water. Faye shucked her beach wrap and immediately a college student whistled loudly.

"I'm too old for you, honey," Faye called over to the young man as she spread out her towel and lay down. "Ah, this is bliss," she said as she stretched out in the hot sun.

Chuck spread his towel and lay down beside her. "Doesn't it make you a little self-conscious that people can see so much?" he asked curiously.

Faye sensed no criticism in the question. "No, not at all. I feel very free about my body, and while I don't feel as if I'm showing it off deliberately, I don't mind if people see me. How about you? Does it bother you when people see your body?"

"Not you, of course," Chuck said. "But I don't think I'd ever feel comfortable on a beach in something like that." He gestured in the direction of a well-built man in a brief bikini.

"That's too bad," Faye murmured. "Because you would look better in it than he does."

"Thanks, hon," Chuck murmured.

Faye closed her eyes and let her mind drift, but after a few minutes her mind could drift to nothing but how hot she was becoming in the afternoon sun. She got up and ran across the warm sand to the cool water that lapped the shores. She'd reached a depth almost to her knees when she felt an arm slide around her waist and her body being lifted. "Chuck, what are you doing?" she squealed.

"Me man from Atlantis," he explained as he strode with her out toward the deeper water. "You mermaid." He stopped in water that was chest deep and dropped her into it.

Faye sputtered as she came to the surface of the cool,

salty water, then gasped as the back of her suit came untied. "Help me, Chuck, quick! I'm losing this suit!"

"Oh, no!" Chuck said as he grabbed for the offending straps. He quickly turned to shield her from the people on the beach as she clutched at the front of the suit and backed up to him. He found the straps in the water and with fumbling fingers tied the narrow strings. "There, what little modesty you have is preserved," he said, only half teasingly.

"All right, all right, so I need a different suit to roughhouse in," Faye griped as they set out for the shore. "Look, I'll make a deal with you. You buy a suit that looks a little less like the turn of the century, and I'll buy a suit to get thrown in the water in. We'll shop in the morning."

Chuck looked down at Faye's swimsuit, then over at his own. "Do you think we can make such a radical change in our life-styles?" he asked.

Faye laughed and said she was willing to make the effort.

They spent part of the afternoon sunning on the beach, then swam a few laps in the pool and had drinks while dangling their feet in the water. Chuck felt uncomfortable with the many appreciative masculine stares Faye received, but he noticed that she seemed oblivious to them and in no way encouraged the attention. In fact, she deftly rebuffed a good-looking man who tried to strike up a conversation with her by smiling widely and telling him she was on her honeymoon.

Chuck was also painfully conscious of the good-looking, sexy men he saw who weren't too self-conscious to wear a revealing swimsuit, or to try to strike up a conversation with another man's companion. What if she found one of them more interesting than him? he wondered. What if she started to find him dull and boring?

The sun was creeping lower in the sky when Faye turned to Chuck. "Think we better go in before we broil?" she asked. "I don't want to get so burned we can't come back out tomorrow."

Chuck downed the last of his drink and nodded. "We ought to shower off some of this sand." They gathered up their towels and walked through the lobby of the hotel to the elevators. "Do you want to have dinner here, or would you rather find a restaurant down the island?"

"I'm sure here will be fine," Faye said as they stepped onto the elevator.

They rode up to their floor with a middle-aged couple. The man couldn't take his eyes off the shapely expanse of leg Faye's towel did not hide. Chuck told himself he was being silly, but he couldn't help feeling jealous of the man's appreciation of Faye's beauty. When he unlocked the door to the hotel room, they both made a beeline for the bathroom.

"Ugh, this sand gets everywhere," Faye complained, pulling down her bikini briefs, dumping them in the sink. Chuck reached out and untied her suit top, and she threw it in on top of the bottoms. "I think I did get sunburned," she said as she twisted around to see her back in the mirror.

Chuck peeled off his trunks and dropped them on top of her suit. "I'll kiss it and make it better," he said, and reached out to caress her shoulder with his lips. She tasted slightly sandy and salty.

Faye shivered with pleasure at the touch of his mouth on her heated flesh. "Would you like to shower off this sand with me?" she asked, knowing what the answer would be.

They had shared many baths and showers since their first night together, and to Faye it had become an important part of their lovemaking.

Chuck nodded and turned on the spray. While they waited for the water to warm up, he wrapped his arms around Faye's gritty body and kissed her, snaking his tongue into her mouth and exploring the sweetness he found there. Then he pulled away and adjusted the spray.

"If we do too much of that we'll get carried away and never get to dinner," he said, and pushed her into the shower stall.

"So what?" Faye asked as he stepped in behind her. "So what if we never get down there?" She wrapped her arms around his body, raised her lips and nibbled the soft flesh of his lower lip. "So what if we make love all evening? It's our vacation, isn't it?"

Chuck nodded as he took her into his arms and possessed her lips in a long, lingering kiss. The depths of Faye's passionate nature never ceased to amaze him. Even Julie hadn't wanted him like this! Without breaking off their kiss, he unwrapped a bar of hotel soap and began to lather Faye's body, starting with her shoulders and her arms. His soapy hands glided over the soft, smooth skin of her arms and then down her chest, where he paid special attention to the gentle rise of her breasts.

Faye gasped when he slid his soapy fingers over the swelling nub of her nipple. She pulled her head back from Chuck's kiss and grinned at him. "I'm getting all clean and you're all dirty," she teased, then unwrapped a second bar of soap. Now, similarly armed, she began a soapy investigation of Chuck's anatomy, starting with his face and shoulders.

They washed each other with gentle and tantalizing fingers, touching and stroking and caressing. Faye stroked the firm flesh of Chuck's waist and hips and ran her hands down the strength of his thighs. He, in turn, caressed the tender skin of her waist and the soft swell of her stomach. His hands drifted lower and stroked the firm flesh of her thighs. Faye soaped her hands again and lovingly caressed his swelling masculinity, delighting when she could feel desire swell it further.

"You know, that sand does get everywhere," she teased when Chuck seemed surprised at her boldness. "Got to make sure we've taken care of it all."

"Yes, I guess you're right," Chuck said innocently, then ran a soapy hand down to a place that wasn't innocent at all. "After all," he teased when Faye gasped, "you did say *everywhere.*"

They touched and caressed while they rinsed the soap from their bodies, then Chuck remembered they hadn't washed their hair and they started all over again, soaping each other's hair and very carefully rinsing. Taking Faye into his arms, Chuck kissed her under the pounding spray, locking his lips with hers in an intimate embrace as their naked bodies entwined under the warm stream of water. They kissed and touched and embraced for long moments, his hard, aroused body pressed against her soft, quivering one. Faye could feel his chest hair against her breasts, the firm muscles of his thighs, and the strength of his desire for her. She was on fire for Chuck, she thought—only *he* could quench the flame that was licking inside her.

Chuck turned off the water and they stepped out of the shower. As they sometimes did, Chuck dried Faye while she dried him, patting one another gently with the soft, velvety towels the hotel provided. Then Chuck pointed to

147

the vanity stool and picked up a wide-toothed comb. "Let me brush out the tangles," he volunteered.

Faye sat down on the stool and Chuck picked up the mass of tangled dark hair and put a towel under it. With sensitive fingers he unraveled the worst of the tangles, carefully working out the snarls, leaving her hair smooth. Then he picked up the blow drier provided by the hotel. "Rapunzel, Rapunzel, let down your ebony hair," he whispered as the warm air blew through her silken tresses.

Faye shivered at the sensation of the warm air and Chuck's tender ministrations. How could he know how to please her so well? she wondered. He worked hard to dry the mass of hair that tumbled down her back, then turned her around and held her by the shoulders as he pulled her up out of the chair.

"Are you ready for me?" he asked.

"Oh, yes, Chuck, I'm ready," she whispered.

Chuck picked her up and carried her out of the bathroom, but when he saw the late-afternoon sun streaming across the bed, he put Faye down and started to close the drapes to the balcony. "Oh, no, Chuck, don't do that," Faye protested.

"But, Faye, the sun's coming in," Chuck said.

Faye sat down in a swath of sunlight. "I don't mind," she said softly.

"But somebody might see," Chuck protested weakly as he observed the way the sun dappled Faye's lovely body.

Faye shook her head. "Nobody will see," she told him. "We're too high up for that. The only creatures that might see us are the sea birds out there, and they won't mind."

Chuck looked out at the wide expanse of foaming water and nodded, then joined Faye in the swath of light. "Let me make love to you," he murmured as he took her into his arms.

Faye turned Chuck so that she was lying half on top of him. "No, let me make love to you," she whispered, and pushed his shoulders into the pillows.

Maybe it was the sun, maybe it was the pounding waves of the ocean, maybe it was the uninhibited atmosphere of the island, maybe it was Chuck himself—Faye didn't know what was driving her, and didn't care. Her desire for Chuck drove her to greater daring than she had ever known with him. She let her lips travel down his body, finding and touching the twin pleasure points of his hard flat nipples, then moving down his body to his navel, where she drew hot wet circles around the indentation. Then she traveled lower, to the hard strength of his masculinity. She touched it tentatively with her lips, pulling back when Chuck murmured a sudden protest. She looked up to find Chuck blushing, and was horrified that no one had ever cared enough for him to give him pleasure in this way.

"Let me, Chuck," she said as her lips returned to their pleasurable play.

She tormented Chuck until he was nearly at the brink, then moved over him swiftly to make them one. Chuck marveled at the unselfish way Faye had brought him pleasure. He looked up at the strong, tender woman who moved over him in the sunlight, her dark hair falling in a curtain around the both of them, and could not believe how good she could make him feel.

Faye moved sinuously, bringing maximum delight to herself and Chuck. She could tell by the tenseness of his muscles that he felt the same strong arousal that she did. Finally, when she thought she could take no more, Chuck arched beneath her and she let herself give way to the waves of passion that overtook them both, crying out as shooting stars went off behind her eyes. Chuck reached out and clasped her shoulders and pulled her down to him.

"I love you, Faye," he said softly.

"And I love you," she returned.

They lay quietly for a while, watching the sun get lower in the sky and the waves flow toward the shore, then showered again and went upstairs to the penthouse restaurant for dinner.

Faye was aware of the striking couple they made as they walked in together, both tall and tanned and attractive. But Chuck, as usual, was oblivious to his own appeal and the appreciative stares he received from the women in the restaurant. They enjoyed huge broiled shrimp dinners, split a piece of pecan pie, then danced to the sensual beat of the Latino band until sexual desire overtook them again.

They were back in their room before midnight. This time they made slow, languorous love in a puddle of moonlight while waves pounded the shore outside.

"Well, are you ready to go shopping for new suits?" Chuck teased Faye after sipping the last of his breakfast coffee.

Faye finished her toast and nodded. "That first, and then can we drive into Brownsville and go shopping at the market? I just love their silver jewelry."

"I'll get you something," Chuck promised.

When they walked out of the coffee shop and into the lobby, Faye approached the desk. "Can you recommend a nice shop where we can pick up a couple of swimsuits?" she asked.

The clerk looked at the well-dressed couple in front of him and decided they would prefer one of the better shops.

"Sure. You can try the Hawaiian Store or the Dune-breakers. They carry the better brands. They're both just down the strip."

Faye thanked the clerk and soon she and Chuck were standing in front of racks of expensive swimwear. She picked out several she thought would be secure in the water and yet were still tantalizing.

"See anything you like?" she asked.

Chuck shrugged. "They're all so bare!" he complained.

"Pick some out and try them on," she said, and headed toward the dressing rooms. A few minutes later she'd settled on a sleek orange maillot that tied around the neck and had mesh inserts down the front and the sides. Secure, but definitely not modest! she thought. She put her clothes back on and knocked on the door to the second dressing room.

"How are you coming?" she asked.

Chuck pushed open the door and let her into the tiny cubicle. "Well, I don't like this one at all," he said. He was dressed in a flashy, low-cut man's bikini that revealed several inches of pale flesh below his waist.

"You look great," Faye said, peering at him. "But it wouldn't stay on any better than my suit did yesterday."

Still, she felt disappointed when Chuck took off the suit and picked up another one. The second was more substantial than the bikini, but the tight briefs left little to the imagination. Chuck peered at himself in the mirror.

"They're great," Faye enthused.

Chuck shook his head. "I don't know," he said as he stared at the portion of his body that the suit hugged tightly. "I just don't feel comfortable in them."

Faye's face fell before she could stop it. "But, Chuck,

everybody wears suits like this one and thinks nothing of it," she protested.

"I'll buy it and I'll try to wear it," Chuck said, vowing not to appear prudish in front of Faye.

Faye reached out and read the price tag. "No, there's no sense in paying thirty-five dollars for a suit you won't even wear. Let me go out there and see what I can find."

She returned a few minutes later with a couple of suits that were little different from the one he'd brought with him. Chuck settled on a blue one, then they paid for their suits and headed back across the causeway toward the mainland.

"Did you have fun in Mexico?" Chuck asked that afternoon as he and Faye were changing into their new suits.

Faye, wiggling into the new suit, nodded. "Yes, and I just love the silver bracelet," she said. She leaned over and kissed Chuck on the cheek. "Thank you."

"And I thank you for this," Chuck said as he held out his hand and stared at the turquoise ring on his finger. "It's the first time a woman has ever bought me a piece of jewelry, other than my wedding ring."

"I'm glad you like it," Faye said, and backed up to Chuck. "Here, will you tie these?"

Chuck tied her straps and stared down at the new suit. It was sexier than the other one had been! Or was it just sexy because Faye wore it? he wondered.

They carried their laundered beach towels to the beach, spread them on the sand, and lay down in the sun, tired from their morning of shopping, Chuck shut his eyes. As he slept, Faye gazed down at him with love in her eyes.

She'd been disappointed when she hadn't been able to persuade him to buy a more revealing suit, but she'd been sorry for his own sake, not hers. If he wanted to bundle up on the beach like an Eskimo, she thought, that was fine with her, but she couldn't help but feel that *he* would be happier if he were less inhibited about his body. But what difference did a swimsuit make, she chided herself, when his lovemaking could turn her bones to water?

Chuck lay facedown, pretending to sleep. He knew Faye was staring at him, and didn't want to see the disappointment in her eyes. She wishes I were less inhibited, he thought. She wishes I were better in bed. She had known yesterday, when she'd caressed him so lovingly, that no one had ever done that to him before. He groaned inwardly: God, how naive he must seem to her!

She needs a more sensual man, Chuck thought sadly as the hot sun burned into his bare back. One who isn't too shy to wear a bikini on a public beach. One who doesn't get embarrassed when she wears a revealing suit or when she dances. One who knows more about what to do in bed. Could he ever become that man? he wondered. He would try, he told himself, but he doubted that he could ever really be the right man for Faye.

CHAPTER EIGHT

"Miss Catalini, did you enjoy the holiday?" Darlin asked as she set a cup of coffee down on Faye's desk.

"Yes, Darlin, it couldn't have been any nicer," Faye said. She picked up the steaming coffee and sipped it carefully so as not to burn her tongue, meanwhile looking at Darlin's sunburned nose. "Looks like you had a good one too."

"Sure did. We went to Astroworld all day yesterday. Had a blast."

"And last night?" Faye teased as Chuck walked in. "Did you and your date have a blast last night too?"

"My date?" Darlin asked, momentarily confused. "Oh, I didn't have a date yesterday. I took a couple of kids from the Children's Home with me. I see these kids, oh, maybe once a week and take them on some kind of outing," she rattled on. "They're good kids, considering the hell they went through at home before the social workers finally took them away from their parents. Well, got to get Mr. Wilson his coffee. How about you, Mr. Goodall? Would you like a cup?"

"I'll get one later," Chuck said as he popped open his briefcase and removed some papers. "Thanks."

"How was your vacation?" Darlin asked.

"Great," Chuck replied. At least most of it was, he

amended. He still couldn't shake his conviction that Faye needed a more uninhibited, dynamic man in her life.

Darlin left the room, her dangling rhinestone earrings swinging around her face, and Faye stared after her. "Can you imagine that girl giving up an afternoon a week to spend time with kids like that?" she asked.

Chuck shook his head. "No, but I think it's good of her." He chuckled under his breath. "I wonder what the kids think of her hair?"

"Oh, they probably want to grow up and be just like her. And they could do a lot worse."

Ray opened Faye's door and poked his head inside. "Hello, hello, how did our local lovebirds enjoy their vacation?" he teased. "How was all that hot sand and sexy moonlight?"

Chuck blushed and Faye glowered at Ray. "Why don't you just write it up on the bulletin board?" she asked him. " 'Faye and Chuck spent the weekend together.' "

"Oh, nobody heard me," he said. He came in and shut the door behind him. "So how was it? Really? Carol and I thought about you while we roasted three-dozen hot dogs for the block party."

"It was considerably better than the block party," Chuck said as he handed Faye a stack of papers.

"Will I see you for lunch, Chuck?" Faye asked.

Chuck shook his head. "I've got a business lunch lined up with a hospital administrator. I'll see you for dinner, though. Your place." He headed out the door, shutting it behind him.

"So we're to the your-place-or-mine stage," Ray said thoughtfully.

Faye nodded and smiled faintly. "Are you really so surprised?" she asked. "After all, you set it up."

"That I did, and I can't help but admit that I'm rather proud of myself for coming up with you for him," Ray said smugly. "Or is it him for you? Anyway, you're both happier than I've ever seen you."

"I am, but I'm not so sure about Chuck. He's still trying to get used to the idea of Fatima, although I think he's almost there. But lately he's been a little quiet and moody." Faye shrugged. "But maybe he's always been that way and I just didn't see it for a while."

Ray shook his head. "No, Chuck's never been moody. Maybe something's bothering him, but I'm sure it's not you. Now, since your knight in shining armor is unavailable to take you out to lunch, will you go with the knave of hearts?"

"Oh, Ray, don't feel like you have to take me out just because Chuck's not going to be able to," Faye protested.

"No, really, Faye, I would love to take you out. I have something I want to talk to you about anyway. A job."

"Oh?" Faye asked, raising an eyebrow. Then she grinned. "Twelve noon, and don't be a minute late!"

Ray was right on time. He and Faye walked through the blistering midday heat to the restaurant where he and Chuck had taken her in April. They'd settled in and the waiter had taken their order when Ray got out a date book and consulted it. "Are you already dancing two weeks from this Thursday night?" he asked.

Faye got out her own date book and checked it. "No, so far I'm free that night. Why? Who wants me to dance?"

"Well, my Kiwanis Club is having Business Night that night. It's the only stag party we have all year, and this year I'm in charge of entertainment. I thought you might beat the barbershop quartet we had last year."

"I'm sure I would," Faye said dryly.

"No, this group wasn't too bad if you listened to the lyrics," Ray laughed. "Remember, it was a *stag* party."

"Oh, I get it," Faye said as she nodded, then a thought crossed her mind and she frowned. "But doesn't Chuck belong to that club too? Won't he be there?"

"Yes, Chuck belongs and he will be there, but what does that have to do with anything?" Ray asked as the waitress set two chef's salads in front of them both.

Faye picked up her fork and tasted the salad. "I'm not sure I should dance in front of his friends like that. Besides, won't some of my business contacts be there?"

Ray chewed on a chunk of turkey. "As far as any of your own contacts being there, absolutely not. That's part of why Chuck and I joined this particular Kiwanis and not one of the others—so we could get away from the people we have to work with."

"And what about dancing in front of Chuck's friends?" Faye asked.

Ray shrugged. "Aw, come on, Faye, dance for us. Who's going to know that you and Chuck are dating? Shoot, with that beauty mark and that makeup you wear, even if you did run into some of them later, they'd never in a million years make the connection. Please, Faye. If you don't do it, we're back to the obscene quartet."

Faye laughed, then nodded in surrender. "All right, I'll dance! Anything to rescue the esteemed Kiwanis from the wicked warblers! So when and where?"

"We're setting up in the banquet room of the Emerson Hotel. How about you showing up at nine?"

Faye wrote the time and the place in her appointment book. "I sure hope Chuck doesn't mind me doing this," she murmured, then Ray asked her a question about tax law, changing the subject completely.

Chuck slammed on the brakes to keep from hitting a small dog, then drove more cautiously toward Faye's condo. He realized he was always in a hurry to see Faye, to have her welcome him eagerly and take him into her arms. But how much longer was she going to go on feeling that way? he wondered. How long was it going to take her to tire of her shy, quiet lover? Stop thinking like that! Chuck warned himself. Stop thinking you're defeated when you're not! He was spoiling their relationship with his doubts and his fears, he thought, but felt powerless to stop himself from being so insecure.

He parked behind Faye's car, then got out and opened Faye's door with the key she'd given him. She was in the kitchen, in a pair of pink running shorts and a matching top that showed off her tan. As she leaned over, removing a pan from the oven, Chuck admired the firm fullness of her bottom. He reached out but Faye shook her head.

"If you swat it, you'll make the cake fall."

Chuck reached out and patted her bottom anyway. "Make it into cookies," he said as Faye straightened with a bubbling casserole between her gloved hands. "You fibbed! There isn't any cake," he complained laughingly.

"Yes, there is, right over there in the bakery box," Faye said.

She set the hot casserole on the stove, took a salad out of the refrigerator, and put it on the table while Chuck set the silverware, then carefully transferred the casserole to the table while Chuck poured them iced tea. Should I tell him now about dancing for his club, or should I wait? she asked herself. She thought a minute and decided to wait until after they'd eaten. Chuck would be more relaxed then, and might take the news better.

Faye thought Chuck seemed distracted during dinner, but since she was wondering how he might feel about her dancing for the Kiwanis, she didn't talk much either. They both ate heartily, and Faye decided that dessert would be the time to break the news. She cut them each a big piece of cake and sat back down.

"Ray took me out to lunch today," she said. "He wants me to dance for your Kiwanis Club."

"Good old Ray, he got stuck with the entertainment this year," Chuck laughed. "What did he say when you told him no?"

"Oh, I didn't tell him no," Faye said. "It took a little wheedling on his part, but he convinced me that it would be all right."

Chuck's fork stopped in midair and he stared across the table at Faye. "You mean he actually persuaded you to dance for *my* Kiwanis Club?" he demanded. "Faye, how could you do that to me?"

"Do what to you?" Faye snapped, annoyed with his response.

"Dance like that in front of my friends," Chuck almost wailed. "Show yourself like that to them."

Faye's eyes narrowed. "I beg your pardon, Charles, but I don't understand just what you mean," she said coldly.

"Just what I said," Chuck replied. "You get up there and the sex just oozes out of you, and you know it. Couldn't you keep that part of yourself private?" *Where my friends can't all see you and want you for themselves? he added to himself. Where one of them might want to try to fill your needs better than I can?*

Faye jumped up out of the chair, her cake forgotten. "Chuck, my dancing is a perfectly natural form of self-expression," she protested. "I'm sorry if you find the dancing too sensual for your taste. But I *am* a sensual person and I can't help it if it shows!" She picked up her cake plate and stomped into the kitchen.

"But do you have to advertise it?" Chuck demanded, following her. "Hell, yes, you're sensual and we both know it! But do you have to put it up on a billboard in front of my friends? Do you have to flaunt it?"

"I'm *not* flaunting it!" Faye yelled in his face. "And if you could tell the beautiful from the lewd, you might be able to see that!"

"Yes, and if you weren't such an oversexed little exhibitionist, you might be able to understand how I feel!" Chuck yelled back. "If you cared anything about me, you'd cancel."

"NO WAY!" Faye roared. "This oversexed little exhibitionist is going to dance for your friends! I'll be damned if I'm going to give in to a prune-faced prude who won't even show off his navel at the beach!"

Chuck whitened and Faye's eyes filled with tears. "That was below the belt, but so was the part about being an oversexed exhibitionist," she said. "Go home, Chuck. If you don't, we'll fight all evening."

Wordlessly, Chuck turned on his heel and left Faye's house. He got into his car and drove slowly home. Why can't she understand what it's like for me when I have to watch other men strip her with their eyes? he thought. Doesn't she know that it terrifies me every time a man looks at Fatima and desires her? Doesn't she know? Or does she know and just not care?

Faye sobbed as she put the dishes into the dishwasher. Doesn't he know how much I love to dance? she asked herself. Mechanically, she shut the dishwasher, set the dial, and left the kitchen. Spotting Chuck's cake plate and utensils, she swore to herself, carried them into the kitchen, and dumped them into the sink. Then she wiped her eyes on a paper towel and sat down in the living room.

Chuck just didn't understand how much she loved to dance. I thought he was getting used to the idea of my being a belly dancer, she told herself. But if his reaction tonight had been anything to go by, he was still as far from accepting Fatima as he'd ever been. Was he always going to be so prim and proper? she wondered. Was he always going to hate the thought of her dancing and what it revealed about her to those who saw her dance?

Faye looked in the mirror and adjusted the uppermost scarf in her bodice. Fatima was ready to dance. She was a little early, so she stared for a moment at Fatima's exotic face in the mirror. Would anyone notice that Fatima looked a little tired? Would anyone notice that she seemed sad?

Faye shrugged and shoved her zills down into her purse. She doubted that the Kiwanians would see anything except the belly dancer they'd hired to dance for them. All except for one Kiwanian, and she had no idea what he would see or how he'd feel. How would Chuck react to her dancing tonight? she wondered. Would he even watch her dance? Would tonight force them out of the state of limbo that their relationship had fallen into?

Chuck had come by to see her the evening after the argument. They had both apologized but had not talked about the problem or dealt with it in a meaningful way, and Faye could feel Chuck withdrawing further and further from her emotionally. They had made love a few times since the argument, but it had been empty and meaningless, and this last week they hadn't even tried. *Oh,*

Chuck, why does it bother you so much that I love to dance? she asked herself as she got into the car and drove toward the Emerson Hotel.

Chuck got a Scotch and soda from the bar and wandered around the various exhibits put up by some of the other Kiwanians, but his mind was not on the business displays or the key chains and coffee mugs his fellow Kiwanians were giving away. Ray had said that Faye was dancing at nine, so he had exactly fifteen minutes to wait until the woman he loved danced for this rowdy crowd. Afterward, he thought, he was going to hear suggestive remarks and wonder if someone would consider approaching Faye tonight or calling her later, as he'd wanted to the first time she'd danced for him. There were a number of single and divorced men in the club whom she might find attractive, he mused, and since they had been so cold and distant recently, Faye might be ready for a new man in her life.

Chuck finished his drink and sat down beside Ray at the table where they were giving out brochures and notepads with Cox and Wilson imprinted on top. "Well, I guess it's about time for Fatima," Ray teased as Chuck checked his watch.

"Wonderful," Chuck mumbled.

"Yes, I can hardly wait for her to get out there and start all those little sexy wiggles and bumps—"

"Shut the hell up, Ray," Chuck snapped, his eyes narrowing dangerously.

Ray's smile faded as he looked into Chuck's furious face. "Say, this is really bothering you, isn't it?" he asked incredulously.

"Hell, yes, it's bothering me!" Chuck shot back. "How would you feel if it were Carol?"

162

Ray opened his mouth to speak, but at that moment the lights went out and the room became hushed. It remained dark for a moment, then pink spotlights above the small dance floor bathed the room in an eerie glow as Fatima stepped onto the postage-stamp-size dance floor. She waited a moment, hands raised above her head, for the music to start, and when the driving, beating sound began her body flew into motion, twisting and jerking her stomach and hips, her body undulating in the soft spotlight of pink.

Faye shut her eyes and commanded her body to move, striving for greater perfection than she'd ever shown as a dancer. While waiting to begin, she'd spotted Chuck sitting beside Ray and knew there would be no way he could keep his eyes off her, in spite of the disapproving frown on his face. She was going to give him and his friends the dance of a lifetime for that frown! she thought, trailing a scarf back and forth in the air before it landed at the feet of one of the Kiwanians. *So you think I'm an oversexed exhibitionist? I'll show you oversexed! This is beautiful, damn your puritan hide, and I'll have you believing that before you walk out of here!*

I can't believe she's dancing like this, Chuck thought as Faye's body twisted and swirled on the dance floor. *What she did for me that time was child's play compared to what she's putting on tonight.*

Chuck stared, mesmerized, as Faye's body undulated to the pounding Eastern rhythm. Then as the music slowed she did, too, moving in graceful harmony. Not a man moved a muscle as Faye twitched her stomach, hips, hands, and shoulders in a beautiful symphony of motion. Chuck's stomach heaved as Faye pulled out scarf after scarf, revealing more of the sexy stomach and waist that he

163

had become so intimately familiar with, her tanned skin gleaming with perspiration in the spotlight. He forced himself to look away from the vision of sensuality in front of him, but was even more uncomfortable when he saw the avid expressions of desire on the faces of many of the men around him. She has them around her little finger and she knows it, he thought.

They're with me tonight, Faye thought as she narrowed her eyes to a slit and slowed her movements to a snakelike writhe. They're loving me tonight. As her zills clapped above her head, Faye slithered and swayed, and as usual she began to forget where she was and whom she was dancing for.

She moved with the provocative beat of the music, her pent-up passion and restlessness exploding suddenly as the music blared into a fast-paced yet sensual storm of sound. Faye bounced and swirled, her scarves flying around her as she shed scarf after scarf until, except for her coins, she was bare from just below her breasts to low on her hips. She took a scarf, raised it above her head and stretched it tight between her hands. At the same time she bent backward, her stomach moving back and forth, until her wildly curling hair brushed the floor. Then she slowly made her way back up, her body never missing a beat even in its unnatural position. When she was upright she raised her hands and beat her zills loudly, waiting for the final crash that would signal the end of her dance. Her head thrown back, her eyes glazed, she danced with a feverish drive that glittered out of her dark eyes. When the final crashing chord came, she collapsed in the middle of the dance floor, her head bent forward in exhaustion.

The Kiwanians sat for a moment, stunned by the force of Fatima's dancing, then the roar of applause rang in

Faye's ears. She raised her head to acknowledge their tribute, smiling and wiping her face as the men whistled and cheered. Faye smiled Fatima's sensual smile at them and took her bows, then she saw Ray extending his arm to her.

"If you'd rather not be mobbed, I'll get your scarves and bring them to you later."

Faye smiled weakly and let him lead her toward the lobby. "I guess they liked it," she said as they walked out of the room of clapping and cheering men.

"Are you kidding?" Ray asked, opening the door that led to the lobby. "Faye, I've seen you dance on a number of occasions, but I have never, and I do mean *never,* seen you dance like that! You brought down the house!"

Faye reached out and touched Ray's arm. "Tell me," she said quietly. "Was it beautiful or was it lewd?"

Ray turned to Faye with a look of astonishment on his face. "Faye, you have to be kidding! It was beautiful! It was more than beautiful! It was sensual, sure, but—" He broke off and his eyes narrowed. "Did a certain rather prim friend of ours say something along those lines?"

"His words were oversexed exhibitionist."

"You wait until I get my hands on that narrow-minded prig!" Ray snapped. He opened the door of Faye's car for her and she got behind the wheel. "Look, I'll give that so-and-so a piece of my mind when I get back in there."

"Oh, don't bother," Faye said. "He can't help the way he is."

"Yes, but he could help hurting you," Ray said. "See you in the morning."

Chuck stood by the bar and drank down a straight Scotch in three gulps while talk of Fatima swirled around him. What could Faye have meant, dancing like that in front of his friends? And now he had to spend the rest of the evening listening to them raving about that wild, sexy woman who had danced for them. Damn her and damn Ray for asking her to dance! he thought. Chuck slammed his empty whiskey glass on the bar and headed out the door, forgetting his display. He couldn't stand another minute of listening to them talk about Faye. He'd decided he was going to give her a piece of his mind for dancing like that.

Faye sat down on the couch with Lenore in her lap and put her head back against the cushions. The dance had taken a lot out of her, and now she thought about getting her costume off, showering, and going to bed. She sighed with fatigue. Thank goodness tomorrow was Friday— she'd have Saturday to rest. But she'd enjoyed dancing for the Kiwanis men, even though she was sure that Chuck was furious. Well, tough, she thought: She was the way she was, and she was tired of apologizing to him for it.

Lenore's ears pricked up, and a moment later Faye heard a key turning in her lock. She stared across the room, Chuck's furious gaze clashing with hers. He slammed the door behind him and sat down across from her.

"Quite a little dance you put on for my friends tonight," he said coldly.

Faye's eyes narrowed. "Yes, that was quite a dance I put on," she said. "It was a beautiful dance and it was a sensual dance. And I'm tired of defending my dancing to you. Now, you tell me, Chuck. Was it beautiful? *Was it?*"

"Of course it was," Chuck admitted angrily. "I never said it wasn't."

"And the Kiwanians loved it, didn't they?"

"Of course they did," Chuck shot back. "The one you

put on for me was the hula compared to what you did tonight."

"Oh, shut up!" Faye snapped. "You'd object if I *did* do the hula. You'd find something ugly or lewd with the way I did it. You wouldn't like the way I did tap or ballet either, would you? I'm tired of defending myself to you. Look, Chuck, we're not arguing about the dancing itself and we both know it. We're arguing about something else entirely."

"We are too arguing about the dancing," Chuck protested. "We're arguing about the way you flaunt yourself in front of other men when you do a belly dance."

Faye shook her head. "No, we're not," she said. "We're arguing about the way *you* feel when I get up there and show that I'm a very sensual woman. You don't like that, do you, Chuck? You don't like it one bit. I threaten you, Chuck." She stood up and looked down at him with her hands on her hips. "You don't like it when I become Fatima, because she threatens your masculinity, doesn't she?"

Faye knew she had struck a nerve. He stood up slowly, towering over Faye in her dancing slippers. "So you think Fatima threatens me, do you? What if I take a little time tonight and come face to face with that threat? You're Fatima now. Why don't I make love to Fatima and see how threatening I find her?"

Before Faye could protest, Chuck reached out and pulled her to him, claiming her lips in a hard, punishing kiss. She choked from the pressure of his mouth on hers, but instead of trying to pull away she raised her arms and curled them tightly around his neck, pulling him toward her and increasing the punishing pressure on their lips. She opened her mouth when Chuck's tongue raked her lips and welcomed his sensual invasion, fencing his tongue with her own as she tasted the Scotch on his breath. *Take me,* she thought as her fingernails raked through his hair. *Take Fatima. She wants you so much.*

Chuck pulled his head back and stared into Faye's face, looking for the revulsion he assumed she'd feel after the way he'd kissed her. But Fatima stared back at him, wild-eyed, her dark mane in flowing disarray, her lips swollen from his kisses. Her arms were locked around his neck, her breasts heaving up and down, and the expression on her face was eager, welcoming.

"Take me, Chuck," she said, her voice husky. "If that's what you want."

"Oh, *yes* I want!" Chuck said, then pulled her head toward his and captured her lips with his own. He wanted this woman—he'd wanted her ever since she had danced for him months ago. And he had to prove it, both to himself and to her. He *wasn't* threatened he told himself. He *could* hold his own with her. He *had* to, or he would lose Faye. He ran feverish fingers through the tangled mass of hair that cascaded down her back and around her face, then stroked the softness of her back.

"I want you, Fatima," he murmured over and over as he covered her face in hot, moist kisses.

"I want you, too, Chuck," Faye breathed hoarsely as she reached up and caressed the hair at his nape.

She encountered the barrier of his collar and with a quick, sure motion stripped the tie from around his neck and threw it on the floor. Chuck shrugged out of his coat and let it fall to the floor, then his questing fingers trailed down her back to the hooks that held her bodice in place. It took him a moment of fumbling to unhook the secure fastening, then the garment was free and sliding from Faye's body. He reached out and slid the bodice from

168

Faye's arms and tossed it on the floor, baring Faye to where the low-cut skirt grazed her hips. She unbuttoned Chuck's shirt and pushed it off his shoulders. He shrugged out of it and let it fall to the floor, but when he reached for the edge of Faye's skirt she shook her head and stepped back.

"You want Fatima, tonight you get her," she said as she stepped up to her stereo and switched on her practice tape.

Chuck watched, fascinated, as Fatima duplicated many of the motions she had made in front of the Kiwanians. She tossed her shoulders, she whirled her hips back and forth, and then started the long, slow undulations in her midsection that wouldn't stay long and slow for very long. Increasing the speed of her movements, her unconfined breasts bounced as her stomach moved in almost miraculous ways. She danced, building Chuck's desire to a fever pitch as desire grew of its own accord within her.

Faye watched as Chuck's face stared at her with longing and desire. This was a fantasy she'd thought about often since they'd met: dancing for him and then making love to him. Throwing her head back, she uttered a low, guttural groan as the music ended. She opened her arms to him and he flew into them, locking his arms around her waist, holding her body still as he tormented her breasts with his eager lips. First one breast and then the other—he touched and tasted and caressed her nipples until they were hard peaks in his mouth.

Faye touched and stroked Chuck's back and chest, loving the feel of his hard muscles under the hair-roughened skin. She found one nipple under the thick hair and tormented it with her fingernail, then lowered her hands until she encountered Chuck's pants. She fumbled a minute with the buckle, then pushed the pants down his legs, his

169

jockey shorts after them. Chuck let go of her long enough to kick off his shoes and socks and pants, then she was back in his arms and he was pushing her down to the couch. He found the zipper that held her skirt together and opened it, easing her skirt and her minuscule bikini panties down her legs and off her body.

Fatima lay back on the cushions of the couch, her eyes almost closed, passion etched on her features. "Love me, Chuck," she whispered hoarsely. "Don't wait any longer."

Chuck didn't wait. He moved over her and with an impatient movement parted her legs and joined their bodies together, the two of them entwined in a wild, passionate coupling like none they had ever known before. Chuck moved rapidly above her, driving deeply within her body, for once unmindful of her pleasure.

Faye, however, was lost in a sensual world of her own, as Chuck made love to her with more passion than she had even dreamed him capable of. Her excitement building rapidly, she reached the mountaintop quickly, crying out her pleasure as Chuck continued to move above her. No sooner had she reached the heights than she felt her excitement growing again, the heaviness of passion pressing down on her midsection as Chuck's own desire built. She gasped as she reached the crest once more, shooting stars going off behind her eyes as her body trembled with delight. Yet the passion within her swelled again, and when Chuck finally reached the top of the mountain, they were able to tumble down together.

Faye shut her eyes and lay back, her chest heaving. She hadn't known such bliss was possible. She had never even dreamed of such pleasure! And Chuck had brought it to her. He was the only man who had made her feel this way, she thought, and the only man who ever could. She opened her eyes and looked up at him, surprised to find him looking at her with a mixture of awe and fear on his face.

Chuck stared down into Faye's face. Yes, she was Faye again, and not Fatima, but this Faye scared the daylights out of him. He had never taken a woman with the kind of cruel passion that he had just shown her, but if her response was anything to go by, she had loved the experience. She had loved the kind of passion he had brought to her tonight, and he couldn't live up to that on a regular basis. She needed someone who could, he thought.

Silently, he rolled off Faye and started to gather his clothes. She sat up and watched, naked and unashamed, as he pulled his clothes and his shoes back on and walked out the door. He looked back at her, a wealth of sadness in his eyes as he stared at the naked beauty on the couch, then shut the door firmly behind him and headed back for his lonely home.

Faye watched him go, hurt puzzlement in her eyes, then gathered up the pieces of her costume and carried them to her bedroom. Why had he just gotten up and left like that, after he'd made such glorious love to her? she wondered. Was he so truly disgusted by her dancing and the passion that it revealed in her that he just couldn't stand her anymore? Oh, Chuck, what's happened to us? she asked herself as she creamed off Fatima's makeup and took off the mole. Is it that you just can't stand me the way I am? She stepped into the shower, letting the tears from her eyes mingle with the water on her face as she washed the glitter out of her hair and down the drain.

CHAPTER NINE

"Ray, have you seen Chuck this morning?" Faye asked as she handed Ray a computer disk with the Galleria accounts on it.

Ray looked up at Faye's tired eyes and shook his head. "No, I haven't," he said, and took the disk from Faye. "Were you looking for him?" Faye nodded. "Was it bad last night? When I got back to the display, Chuck had left and I figured he went to your place."

"Yeah, I guess it was bad," Faye said, blushing, remembering that part of it wasn't bad at all. "He was pretty upset."

"I still intend to talk to him," Ray said. "His attitude is inexcusable."

"Oh, Ray, I guess he just can't help it," Faye said tiredly. "I didn't really need to see him on business, I just wanted to talk to him for a minute." She picked up the telephone and buzzed Darlin at the reception desk. "Darlin, have you seen Mr. Goodall this morning?" she asked. "He did what? Oh. Well, thanks." Faye put down the telephone. "He called in sick this morning. Darlin said he sounded a little funny."

"People who are sick usually do," Ray said.

Faye bit her lip. "Should I go over to his place tonight and check on him?" she asked. "Do you think he'd mind?"

"You mean, does he want to see you?" Ray asked. "I don't know. Maybe not, if the row was bad. Look, why don't I go over there and check on him tonight? While I'm there I'll try to talk some sense into him. Then I'll call you."

"Thanks, Ray," Faye said. "I'm worried about him."

Faye spent the rest of the day fretting about Chuck, wondering if he was seriously ill and needed a doctor, but she was too unsure of her welcome to call him. She had a dancing job that evening that for once received only half her attention, and then she sat up until one in the morning waiting for a call from Ray. The next morning she was up by nine, and as soon as she thought it a decent hour she called Ray.

"What's wrong with Chuck?" Faye demanded when Ray's distracted voice answered the telephone.

"Uh, I don't know, he wasn't at home last night," Ray panted.

"Are you going over there today?" she asked. "I'm worried about him."

"Uh, sure," Ray said breathlessly.

"Ray, are you all right?" Faye asked.

Faye could hear the sound of Carol's voice whispering in the background. "Hurry up, Ray, and hang up the phone! We only have a little while before the cartoons are over."

"Oops! 'Bye," Faye said, blushing as she hung up the telephone.

She envied Ray and Carol their happy marriage all day as she waited to hear from Ray. Finally giving up on Ray about four, she dialed Chuck's number, but he didn't answer. Well, maybe that was good, she thought as she hung up the telephone. He must be feeling better if he was up and about. She decided to call him later.

Faye dialed Chuck's number again at five, and at six, and every hour thereafter until midnight, at which time she gave up and went to bed. She huddled under the covers in a ball of misery, trying to imagine where Chuck could be. Unable to sleep, she stared out the window most of the night, falling into a restless slumber just as the gray light of dawn began to touch the trees outside her window.

She slept a few hours, then got up and went to a late morning mass. When she got home, she reached for the telephone but hung up before she was halfway through Chuck's number. No, she wouldn't call him today, she thought. He obviously wanted to be left alone.

She put on the skimpy bikini she'd bought for the Padre Island vacation and spent the afternoon at the condominium pool, soaking up the sun and trying not to think about Chuck while she devoured the latest best-selling mystery novel. It was late in the afternoon by the time she finally discovered that it was the maiden aunt who had done it, and her mind was still on the story when she walked up her front sidewalk, her beach towel over her arm, and found Ray sitting on her front porch.

"Ray, how are you?" she called. "Have you seen Chuck?"

Ray raised his head, and Faye gasped when she saw the huge purple bruise that surrounded his right eye. "Our prim and proper friend has a hell of a left hook," he said, touching the tender skin under his eye.

Faye rushed up and peered down into Ray's swollen eye. "Chuck did that to you?" she demanded. "I don't believe it!"

Ray stood up and waited while Faye fumbled with her key. "And this is after holding an ice bag on it half the night last night," he said as Faye unlocked the front door.

He followed her in. "Carol's hacked off at both me and Chuck. Go put some clothes on. I want to talk to you about him."

"You mean I don't get to watch cartoons with you?" Faye teased.

Ray shook his head and grinned wickedly. "If Chuck did this to me for just trying to talk to him about you, I'd hate to see what he'd do to me if I touched you!"

Faye quickly rinsed off in the shower and slipped into a pair of jeans and a T-shirt, then she went into the living room and accepted a glass of iced tea that Ray had made while he waited.

"So what happened to make Chuck slug you like that?" she asked as she sat down across from Ray. "That just isn't like him at all!"

"No, I guess it isn't when he's sober," Ray said, grinning to himself. "But he sure wasn't sober when he laid this one on me! He's been on a bender since Thursday night. He finally passed out last night about ten. I took him home and put him to bed and shut off the phone."

"You're kidding!" Faye exclaimed. "Not Chuck!"

"Yes, Chuck. Yes, Faye, good old prim, proper Chuck was so drunk last night that he could hardly stand up by himself. I don't know how much booze he's been through, but I wouldn't light a match to his breath for a week!"

"Ray, that's terrible!" Faye exclaimed.

"Naw, it's not. I think it's great," Ray chortled. "I didn't know Chuck had it in him."

"You men and your adolescent rites of passage," Faye grumbled.

"But I didn't come over here to show off my great shiner," Ray said. "Apparently you, my dear, were the

175

inspiration for Chuck's little episode." His face sobered. "What happened, Faye?"

"What do you think happened, Ray?" Faye asked bitterly. "He just can't accept my dancing. He can't accept the thought that I'm not prim and proper like him." She turned tear-filled eyes on Ray. "Why did you throw us together, Ray? It's your fault we're hurting today."

Ray fingered his sore eye. "Yes, Chuck said the same thing right before he punched me. I just honestly thought you'd be good for each other."

"But couldn't you tell that we're just not suited?" Faye asked softly.

"Are you kidding? You two are perfect for one another!" Ray declared. "Even Carol thinks so."

"The oversexed exhibitionist and the local prig? You and Carol are going to have to explain yourselves."

"All right, on the surface you two may seem to have some differences, but those differences are complementary ones, Faye. He's prim and proper and needs someone to draw him out a little, help him loosen up, but do it in a gentle way. You are just the person to do that, Faye."

"That's what Celeste said," Faye murmured. "Only what if he doesn't want to be loosened up?"

"Then you work just a little bit harder at it," Ray said. "As for you, my dear, you need to come down off that frenetic merry-go-round you call a life-style and enjoy a little peace and serenity every so often. Chuck could help you do it if you'd only let him."

Faye shrugged. "It sounds good in theory, but it just isn't working, Ray. He can't stand the dancing."

"Did you ever stop and ask him, Faye?" Ray asked softly. "Did you ever ask him *why* it bothers him so much?"

"No, I never did," she admitted. "I accused him of something once, but I never asked."

"Then why don't you ask him?" Ray asked. "I just left him a couple of hours ago. He's sober now, as hung over as hell, but you could talk to him."

"I-I don't think so," Faye said.

"I think you should go," Ray said. He drained the last of his tea and stood up. "After all, what have you got to lose?"

Faye walked Ray to the door, then she sat down on her couch. Maybe Ray was right, she thought. What did she have to lose by going to see Chuck? At the worst, he could tell her that he just couldn't accept her the way she was, that the wild side of her was just too much for him. It would hurt, but at least she would know where she stood.

More likely, he would tell her that he just couldn't accept the dancing, she told herself. Could she give up the dancing that had meant so much to her? Faye sighed and walked to the bedroom closet where she stored her belly dancing costumes. She opened the closet and fingered a gauzy scarf that was looped around a clothes hanger. Yes, she could do it. If Chuck simply couldn't live with the dancing, she would be able to give it up. *Good-bye, Fatima,* she thought wistfully.

Faye picked up her car keys and her wallet and was soon pulling into Chuck's driveway, armed with a bag of groceries. She rang the doorbell and waited patiently, but when a couple of minutes had passed and Chuck had not answered she rang the bell again. She was about to ring it a third time when Chuck threw open the door and stared down at her. He was dressed only in a pair of jeans and had a towel draped around his neck. There were razor nicks on his neck and his hair was damp.

"Faye, what are you doing here?" he asked.

Faye frowned and clicked her tongue at his sallow face and the deep circles under his eyes. "I came to fix you supper, but you've got to promise me you won't slug me in the eye."

Chuck grimaced as he stepped aside to let her in. "God, don't remind me. I'm never going to live that down."

"Oh, Ray's delighted," Faye said dryly. She made her way through Chuck's messy living room to his cluttered kitchen. "Did you spend the weekend here?"

"Part of it," Chuck admitted, and dropped the towel on the counter. "Do you happen to have a couple of aspirins in that sack?" he asked. "I feel horrible."

Faye reached in the sack and handed him a new bottle of aspirin. "Did you take all yours today?" she asked.

Chuck nodded as he cracked open the protective seal. He took out three, downed them with a glass of water, and sat down on a stool. "I don't know why you're here after the way I treated you last Thursday, but thanks."

"I think we both know why I'm here," Faye countered. "If you feel up to picking up a little of that mess in the living room, I'll cook something your stomach can tolerate, and then we've got to talk."

Chuck got up off the stool and took a paper sack from under the sink. Faye could hear him out in the living room while she sliced the ham and beat the eggs for omelets. She poured a couple of glasses of milk and was just dishing up the second omelet when Chuck reappeared with a sack of empty TV dinner trays and beer cans.

He looked down at the omelets and sniffed. "Smells good," he said.

They sat down across from one another. Faye watched as Chuck ate his omelet, and when that one was gone, and

178

he said it was the first food he had eaten all day, she offered to make him another. He finished the second omelet and two more glasses of milk, and together they loaded the dishwasher and straightened the cluttered kitchen. Then Chuck took Faye by the hand and led her into the now-straightened living room and seated her in the low-slung chair across from the couch. He sat down on the couch.

Faye bit her lip as she prepared to say the words she thought would cost her dearly. "Do you think you can accept me as a person, or am I just too wild for you?" she asked.

Chuck stared straight into her eyes. "Of course I love you as a person. And you aren't really all that wild."

Faye's face softened. "I love you too," she said. "If that's the case, I'm willing to give up the dancing. I do love you, Chuck, and I'm willing to do whatever it takes to salvage this relationship."

Chuck shook his head, his face mirroring his sadness. "No, Faye, I would never ask you to give up your dancing. That would be like cutting off your right arm."

"Not really," Faye lied.

"Yes, it would, and we both know it," Chuck said. "Although I certainly appreciate the offer." He reached out and stroked the side of her face. "You must love me very much to make an offer like that."

"I *do* love you, Chuck," Faye said. "And I'm willing to do whatever I can to make our relationship work."

"I know that," Chuck replied softly, looking into Faye's eyes, seeing the love shining from them. "Believe me, if I thought that your quitting dancing would make everything all right, I'd go help you toss out your costumes! But it really doesn't make any difference whether or not you're dancing."

179

"Then why has the dancing bothered you so much?" Faye finally got up the courage to ask. "If you don't think my giving it up will help, then why has it bothered you so?"

"Oh, Faye, let's be honest with ourselves for once," Chuck sighed. "The dancing's not the problem. You're not the problem. I am."

Faye's eyes widened. "How's that, Chuck?"

Chuck stood up and clasped his hands in front of him as he walked across the living room floor. He turned around slowly and faced Faye. "Tell me, did you like it the other night when I made love to Fatima?"

Faye shrugged. "In a way I did. If we hadn't been angry, I would have loved it."

Chuck nodded and shoved his hands in his pockets, then came back to the couch and sat down. "Faye, that's the only time in my life I've ever made love like that."

"I should hope so," Faye said dryly.

"No, really!" Chuck stopped and swallowed. "I'm not a very sexy man, Faye. Julie used to tell me that I was old meat-and-potatoes Chuck, and I guess I am. I'm kind of ordinary, and I imagine that making love to me is dull." He cleared his throat to keep his tears from clogging them. "You're such a sensuous woman, Faye. You're my sensuous enchantress, did you know that? From the first moment I saw you, I was enchanted by your sensuality, your uninhibited spirit, that wild side of you—all the qualities I wish I had. And then, when we started making love and you were so warm, so responsive—"

He got up and paced the floor again, then turned to her with tears in his eyes. "I can't satisfy you as a woman, Faye. You need more than I can give to you. You need a dynamic man, a man who can set your body on fire." He

180

reached up to wipe a tear off his cheek. "A man who would bring your sensuality to life."

"Oh, Chuck," Faye breathed as she stood up and walked across the floor. "Would you like to see the man who brought my sensuality to life?" Chuck shook his head, but Faye took him by the shoulders and turned him around to look in the mirror over the couch. "Look, Chuck. There he is. There's the man who brought me to life."

Chuck stared at his reflection in the mirror.

"Do you really think I'm like that with everyone?" Faye asked as she stood behind him, her hand on his shoulder. "Did you really think I was always that responsive? Well, I wasn't. I used to think there was something wrong with me."

Chuck stared at her reflection in the mirror and she blushed. "Well, I liked it all right, but I kept wondering if that was all there was. And then you came along, and took me into your arms, and for the first time I found out what it was all about." She lowered her eyes. "I figured it was always that good for you, so I didn't say anything about it. I was too embarrassed to admit that it hadn't always been like that for me."

Chuck turned around and held her by the shoulders. "You mean it's me? The man I've been so jealous of is really me?" He held her to him and stroked her hair. "No, Faye, it hasn't always been like that for me. I thought it was always like that for you. I've been scared to death of you, thinking that sooner or later you were going to decide that you needed more than I could give you."

"Oh, Chuck, I wish you knew just how much you have given me," Faye said as she put her arms around his neck. "I knew that I had to be a sensual woman, or I could never have danced like I do, but you were the key that unlocked that sensuality, Chuck. Quiet, gentle you. I liked making love like we did the other night, but I like the other more." She reached up and brushed his lips with her mouth. "I liked it better when you were gentle and strong." She kissed his lips again.

"Then why did you try so hard to get me to buy that sexy swimsuit?" Chuck asked. "I was sure I embarrassed you with my modesty, and I was sure I wasn't sexy enough for you."

Faye shook her head. "It's what goes on behind closed doors that counts as far as sexy goes, and I can assure you that you are plenty sexy! I've never had a man like you in my bed before."

Faye smiled to herself when she could feel Chuck straighten with pride. "And the other—as far as I'm concerned, I couldn't care less what you do or don't wear on the beach. But I really think you would be happier if you were a little looser, more relaxed." She reached out and touched Chuck's bare chest. "Like you are tonight. You haven't given your lack of a shirt a second thought, and neither have I."

Chuck smiled down at her. "We'll work on that some," he said as he sat down on the couch and pulled her down beside him. "And we'll work on teaching you how to relax too." He reached out and circled her lips with his tongue. "Now, is that uninhibited, or is that uninhibited?"

"I think it's very relaxing," Faye teased.

Chuck held her face between his hands and kissed her lightly. "All my fears were for nothing," he said, more to himself than to her.

Faye reached up and stroked the side of Chuck's face. "Will you mind if I dance some?" she asked.

"No more than six times a week, but you can do it twice

182

on Saturdays," Chuck teased. "No, really, I want you to keep dancing. Now that I know that I do give you pleasure that way, I won't mind if the world sees just how sensual you are." He shook his head. "I still can't believe I'm the man!"

Faye reached up and pulled his head down for a long, lingering kiss. "You better believe it," she murmured. "And if it weren't for your hangover I'd prove it to you."

Chuck nibbled the side of her face as he reached down and started to pull her T-shirt out of the waistband of her jeans. "What hangover?" he asked.

"Chuck, you're in no shape to make love right now!" Faye laughed as he whipped her T-shirt over her head. "You've had a headache all day!"

"But that was when I didn't know that I'm the only guy who can ring this certain very sexy lady's bell," Chuck explained. He unhooked her bra and tossed it across the room. "Now that I know, I could run up the side of a mountain, I could swim across the ocean, I could slay three hundred dragons, I could—"

"I can think of a better use for all that energy."

Faye laughed as she pulled off his glasses. She covered Chuck's lips with her own, seeking and sampling the sweetness she found there. Chuck groaned and opened his mouth to hers, their tongues mingling for long moments. Chuck's hands slid down Faye's bare shoulders and found the soft swell of her breasts, which he caressed with the tips of his fingers until they were hard with desire.

Faye moaned and arched her breasts closer to him. "Oh, Chuck, you don't know how wonderful you make me feel," Faye whispered when Chuck finally released her lips.

"Am I really the one, Faye? Am I really the only one that ever made you feel this way?"

"Oh, Chuck, *yes,*" she moaned as his lips drifted down her neck. He touched and tasted the tender skin there, then pushed Faye onto the cushions and loomed over her, settling his weight to one side of her. He tenderly sampled the valley between her breasts, and then singled out one of her nipples to touch and caress. Faye moaned and arched herself closer to his tender lips and tongue, reveling in the spasms of pleasure shaking her body.

"That feels so wonderful," she whispered as her body writhed involuntarily beneath him.

"I feel pretty wonderful too," Chuck whispered, then he shifted his body and covered her lips with his own.

Faye's breasts were crushed against the soft, curling hair on Chuck's chest and the hard muscles underneath, and the weight of his body was a delightful sensation on hers. She ran her hands up and around Chuck's shoulders. They kissed and caressed on the narrow couch, then Chuck twisted his body toward the edge of the couch and rolled their entwined bodies off it, landing with Faye on top of him on the soft shag carpet.

"That couch was too narrow for what I have in mind," he said, and pushed Faye so she settled beside him on the carpet.

"Yeah, I guess it's time we made it to the bedroom," Faye breathed as she nuzzled the bare skin of Chuck's chest.

"No way!" Chuck said as he reached up and pulled a couple of pillows off the couch. "I don't want to take the time to go back there." He unzipped her jeans and pulled them from her body. "Besides, my bedroom's too prim and proper for what I have in mind for tonight."

"Well, all right," Faye said as Chuck stripped the bikini panties from her body. "But I have a feeling that your bedroom's going to have a lot to get used to in the near future!"

"That is so right," Chuck said, and covered her lips in a long, lingering kiss that left Faye breathless.

He quickly stripped his jeans and underwear from his body, but instead of the heated coupling Faye had expected, he pushed her down onto the carpet and lay beside her. "Did you know that I had fantasies for weeks about making love to Fatima?" he asked as his hand caressed the soft skin of her stomach.

Faye shook her head. "No, I didn't," she said. "Although I'm not surprised. How did reality seem compared to the fantasy?"

Chuck shut his eyes and savored the memory. "It was glorious. Wonderful. But not something I could do every day."

"Neither could I," Faye told him softly. "Nor would I want to. I like tenderness and gentleness as well as passion."

Chuck kissed her lips and caressed her hip with his hand. "I have another fantasy," he confessed as Faye wound her arms around his neck.

"Nothing too kinky, I hope," she murmured as his lips caressed the sensitive skin of her temple. "I didn't notice any whipped cream in the refrigerator."

Chuck laughed softly. "No, nothing like that," he said, removing Faye's hands from around his neck. "I've dreamed of having you just lie still and let me love you in any way I wanted to," he said, and bent his head to graze the tip of her breast with his lips. "You wouldn't touch me, but you would let me do anything to you, for as long as I wanted to."

"That sounds like a lovely fantasy," Faye said as she

185

made herself stop touching Chuck. "I think we ought to make that one a reality. As long as I get to try the same thing with you."

"You can try that one out tomorrow night," Chuck promised. He sat up and stared at Faye's outstretched body. At first he did not touch her, but merely caressed her lovingly with his eyes, going over each feature of her face, then searching the tender curves of her shoulders, the ripe buds of her breasts, the softness of her hips and thighs. Then his hands caressed her softly, intimately, starting with the curves of her shoulders and working down her body, touching and stroking her breasts, her stomach, her hips. Faye had to fight not to reach out and touch Chuck as he was touching her, but she knew that she would have her chance tomorrow night. She gasped with pleasure as Chuck slipped his hand between her thighs and stroked the warmth of her femininity, and she was sure that he meant now to make them one.

But no. While still touching her intimately, he began a third journey down her body, this time with the tenderness of his lips and tongue. Slowly, sensuously, he explored her face and neck, her breasts, the soft swell of her stomach, the roundness of her hips. Faye squirmed and writhed under the sensual inspection of her body, but Chuck shook his head as she started to raise her arms and take him to her. She lowered her arms and gave herself over to the storm of sensation building within her. Again she thought that Chuck was about to join with her and make them one.

But she was wrong again. Chuck pushed her knees apart, but instead of joining their bodies together, he continued the intimate inspection of her body with his tongue and lips. Faye gasped at the bold intimacy of his touch, as he brought to her a unique pleasure that she had never known before.

"Oh, Chuck, Chuck," she whimpered as she could feel the spiraling tension tighten her lower body. She felt the pressure become greater and greater, and knew that the moment was near. "Oh, Chuck, *Chuck!*" she called out as the explosion of delight overcame her, splintering her into a thousand pieces.

"I love you, Faye," Chuck said as he moved over her and swiftly made them one.

As before, Faye felt the heat of passion overcome her once again, and eagerly gave herself up to Chuck's embrace. They moved together, Chuck pouring his love for Faye into every move that he made. She could feel herself soaring, spiraling to greater heights.

"I love you, Chuck," she murmured in cadence to the primitive rhythm they set.

Chuck's voice softly called out her name as she felt herself over the edge once again, then with a powerful shudder he joined her on that free fall of pleasure.

They collapsed in a damp tangle of arms and legs, Faye's arms looped tenderly around Chuck's neck. "Am I allowed to touch you now?" she asked.

Chuck nodded. "I love you so much, Faye," he said as he settled down beside her.

"How did that fantasy compare to reality?" she asked.

"Reality was better," Chuck said, grinning wickedly. Then his face softened. "And that's one fantasy we could live pretty often. So when are you going to marry me?"

Faye pushed herself up and leaned on her elbow. "That's a pretty big step. Are we ready to take it?"

Chuck ran his hand down her side. "I think so. Goodness knows, we love each other enough. And besides, you *know* how proper I am!" he teased. "I'm much too inhibited to live with a woman I'm not married to!"

Faye laughed out loud and sat up, crossing her legs in front of her. "Yes, I can just see the look on Gladys's face the next time she comes down for a visit. Chuck, I would be delighted to marry you," she assured him as her eyes began an intimate inspection of his body.

"Faye, what are you doing?" Chuck asked as she continued to stare down at him.

"I decided not to wait until tomorrow to live out my fantasy," she said, and touched his shoulders with the tips of her fingers.

Faye Catalini Goodall stood at the mirror in her new bathroom and stared at the exotic image that looked back at her. I guess married belly dancers don't look any different than single ones do! she thought to herself as she carefully fixed Fatima's beauty mark on her face. She glanced down at the beautiful gold band with the lovely marquise diamond on her finger. No way would she take it off, even to dance! she told herself.

Faye slipped on the wide silver bracelet Chuck had bought her in Matamoros and checked the watch lying on the bathroom counter. Chuck, where are you? she wondered. He'd promised to come and see her dance that night, but it was time for her to leave and he still wasn't home yet. Faye's brow wrinkled in a concerned frown as she turned off the light and walked through the luxurious bedroom of their lovely new home and tax deduction. Had Chuck at the last minute felt he couldn't watch her dance after all? she wondered.

Faye locked the door behind her and checked the address where she was supposed to dance, the cool October air ruffling her wildly curling hair as she got in her car. She and Chuck had been married for a month now; it had been the happiest month of her life, and until tonight she'd assumed he was secure enough in his masculinity and the pleasure he gave her that she could continue to dance as Fatima with no problem. But now that he had not shown up, she had some doubt. Did her dancing still bother him?

Faye found the house where she was supposed to dance, parked her car in front, and waited patiently in the entry for a few minutes until it was time for her to dance. Maybe Chuck just had to work late, she thought. He would watch her dance another time. At least she hoped so.

The lights in the large living room dimmed. As Faye danced into the room the haunting rhythm of the dance took over and she was caught up in the sensual beat of the music. But tonight she sensed a difference in her dancing. Before, her dancing had been the only real expression of her sensual nature. But now that Chuck had opened another avenue of delight to her, she could feel herself taking the sensuality that he had brought to her and incorporating it into her dancing, the result being a symphony of beauty that even she hadn't shown before. Oh, Chuck, I wish you had seen me tonight, she thought as she whirled for the elderly man who was having his birthday party tonight.

The music ended. Amid whistles and cheers Faye leaned down and chastely kissed the elderly man on the cheek, much to his delight. She could hear a commotion behind her, but she did not realize that anything was out of the ordinary until she turned and saw a tall, turbaned sheikh, his face concealed by a scarf, striding across the room. What on earth? she wondered before spotting a familiar pair of horn-rimmed glasses under the scarf and smiling wickedly.

Without saying a word, the sheikh picked her up and strode across the room and out the door with her. The sound of clapping and cheering followed them all the way out the door and almost to the car. Faye pulled down the concealing scarf and slid her arms around Chuck's neck.

"What are you doing?" she demanded as Chuck put her down beside her car.

"I'm kidnapping you," he said cheerfully. "I think the act needs a little zinger at the end." He stared down at Faye in the pale light of the moon. "I've never seen you dance so beautifully, Faye. Could it be that I brought some of that sensuality to you?"

Faye nodded. "I'm glad you could tell," she said.

Chuck lowered his lips and kissed her long and lovingly, then put her into her car and promised to meet her at home in ten minutes. As Faye watched her sheikh walk down the block to his own car, she sniffed back tears of happiness. Now she was sure. Chuck not only *could* accept her many facets and love all of them, it looked as if he were developing a few of his own. Faye wiped a tear of joy out of her eye and started her car. *I'm going to be his sensuous enchantress forever,* she vowed, then followed Chuck's car down the street, toward home.